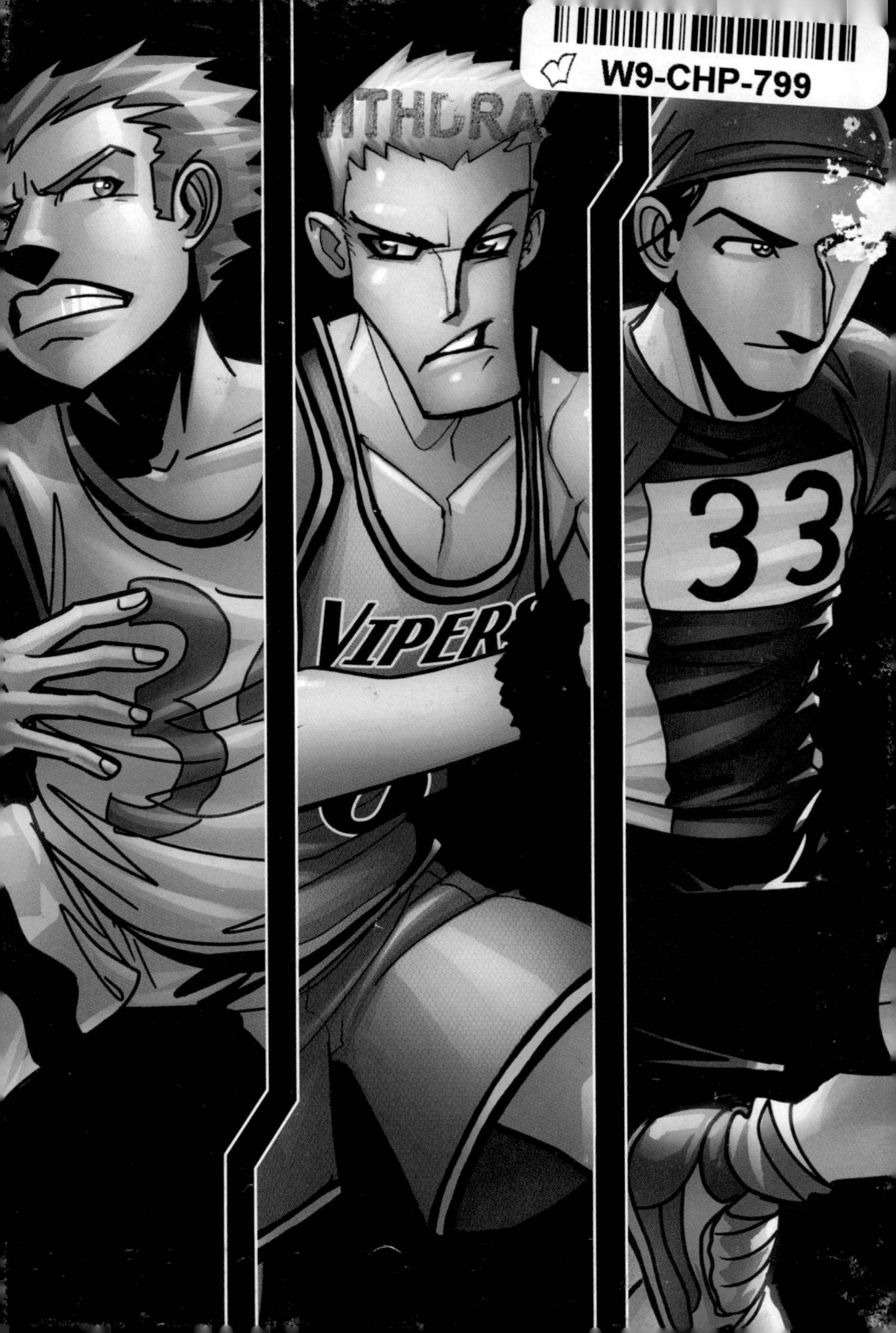
VIPERS
33

UP NEXT ›››

Sports Illustrated KIDS

:02 SPORTS ZONE SPECIAL REPORT

:04 FEATURE PRESENTATION:

HOOP RAT

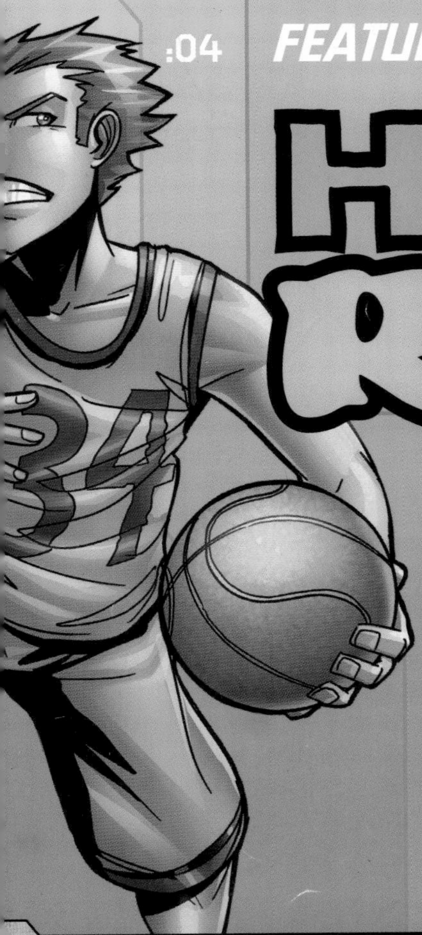

FOLLOWED BY:

:50 SPORTS ZONE POSTGAME RECAP

:51 SPORTS ZONE POSTGAME EXTRA

:52 SI KIDS INFO CENTER

FORMER GOLIATHS TEAM CAPTAIN JOINS SPARTANS SQUAD SIK TICKER

SPORTS ZONE

SPECIAL REPORT

BBL
BASKETBALL

PNT
PAINTBALL

FBL
FOOTBALL

BSL
BASEBALL

SOC
SOCCER

HKY

TEAMMATES NERVOUS ABOUT NEWEST SPARTAN

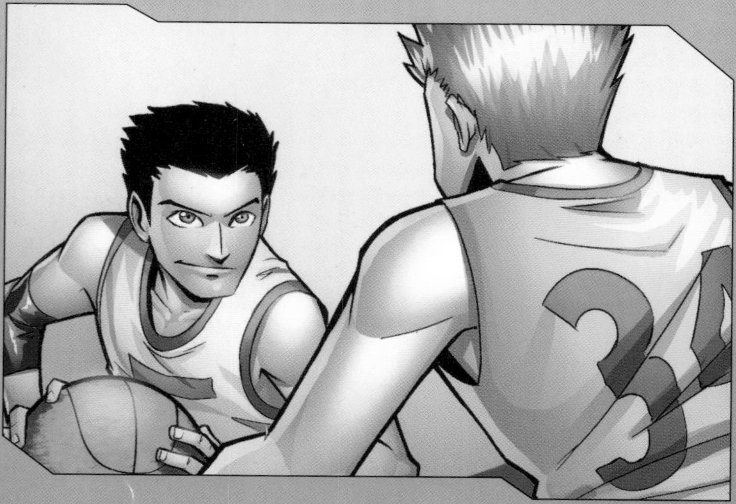

TREY McTIERNAN

STATS:
AGE: 14
POSITION: GUARD

BIO: Trey McTiernan and Max Kendricks will definitely send the already surging Spartans right into the playoffs — that is, if they can learn to trust their new teammate, Griffin Henshaw. Trey isn't convinced that Griff's loyalty lies with the Spartans — he is the former team captain of the Goliaths, who just so happen to be the Spartans' biggest rivals. Trey's facing some tough choices in the coming season . . .

Sports Illustrated KIDS

UP NEXT: HOOP RAT

GRIFFIN HENSHAW

AGE: 14

POSITION: GUARD

BIO: Griffin wasn't happy that his family had to move — his teammates on the Goliaths are also his best friends, so leaving them was doubly painful for the talented teen. He was also the Goliaths' team captain, which has more than a few of his new teammates nervous about him joining their squad.

BLZ vs BHS	3-1
TGR vs ROR	33-32
EAG vs BAN	14-7
SPA vs WLD	4-3
BAN vs ROR	21-15
RZR vs LIG	4-3
BLZ vs BHS	3-1

COACH SCHUSTER

AGE: 47

BIO: Coach "Schu" used to play bass guitar for a well-known rock band. He loves basketball just as much as music.

COACH SCHU

MAX KENDRICKS

AGE: 14   POSITION: FORWARD

BIO: Max thinks that trust is earned, not given — and that Griffin will have to work hard to gain the Spartans' loyalty.

KENDRICKS

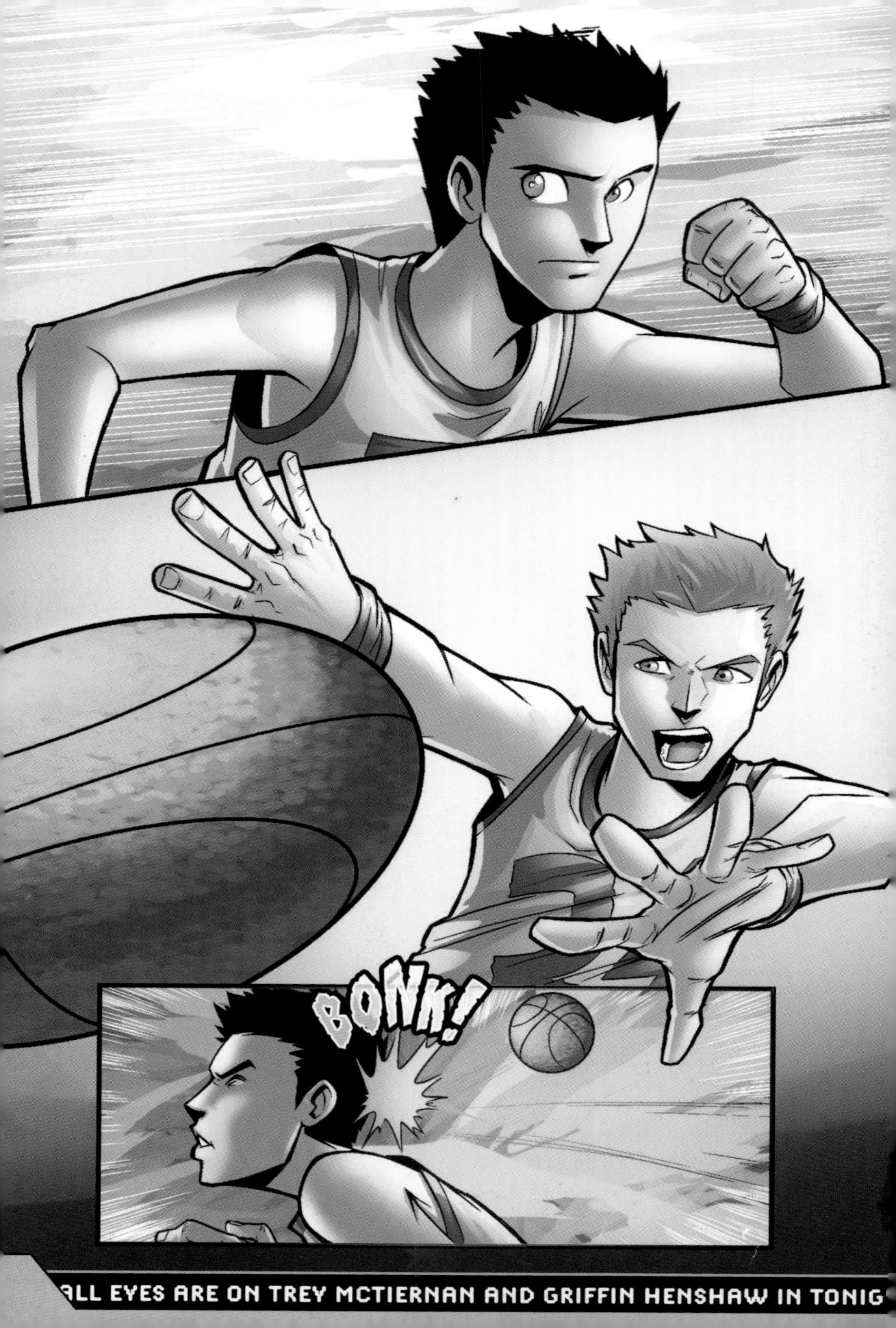
BONK!
ALL EYES ARE ON TREY MCTIERNAN AND GRIFFIN HENSHAW IN TONIG

Sports Illustrated KIDS

PRESENTS

HOOP RAT

A PRODUCTION OF

STONE ARCH BOOKS
a capstone imprint

written by Scott Ciencin
illustrated by Aburtov
penciled by Fernando Cano
inked by Andres Esparza
colored by Fares Maese

Sports Illustrated KIDS *Hoop Rat* is published by Stone Arch Books, 1710 Roe Crest Drive, North Mankato, Minnesota 56003.
www.capstonepub.com

Printed in the United States of America in North Mankato, Minnesota.
052015 008968R

designed and directed by Bob Lentz
edited by Sean Tulien
creative direction by Heather Kindseth
editorial management by Donald Lemke
editorial direction by Michael Dahl

Summary: Trey, the Spartans' team captain, becomes fast friends with Griffin, the newest member of their squad. The problem is, Griff used to play for the Spartans' biggest rivals, the Goliaths, and the rest of the Spartans think he's a rat. Trey doesn't know what to do. His teammates want him to betray his friendship with Griff to save their season . . . but if they're wrong about Griff, then Trey will end up being the rat.

Library of Congress Cataloging-in-Publication Data
Ciencin, Scott.
Hoop rat / written by Scott Ciencin ; illustrated by Aburtov, Cano, Fernando, Esparza, Andres and Fares Maese.
p. cm. -- (Sports Illustrated kids graphic novels)
ISBN 978-1-4342-2223-7 (library binding)
ISBN 978-1-4342-3069-0 (paperback)
ISBN 978-1-4342-4947-0 (e-book)
1. Graphic novels. [1. Graphic novels. 2. Basketball--Fiction.] I. Aburto, Jesus, ill. II. Esparza, Andres, ill. III. Maese, Fares, ill. IV. Title.
PZ7.7.C54Ho 2011
741.5'973--dc22 2010032813

ETBALL SHOWDOWN BETWEEN THE GOLIATHS AND SPARTANS SIK TICKER

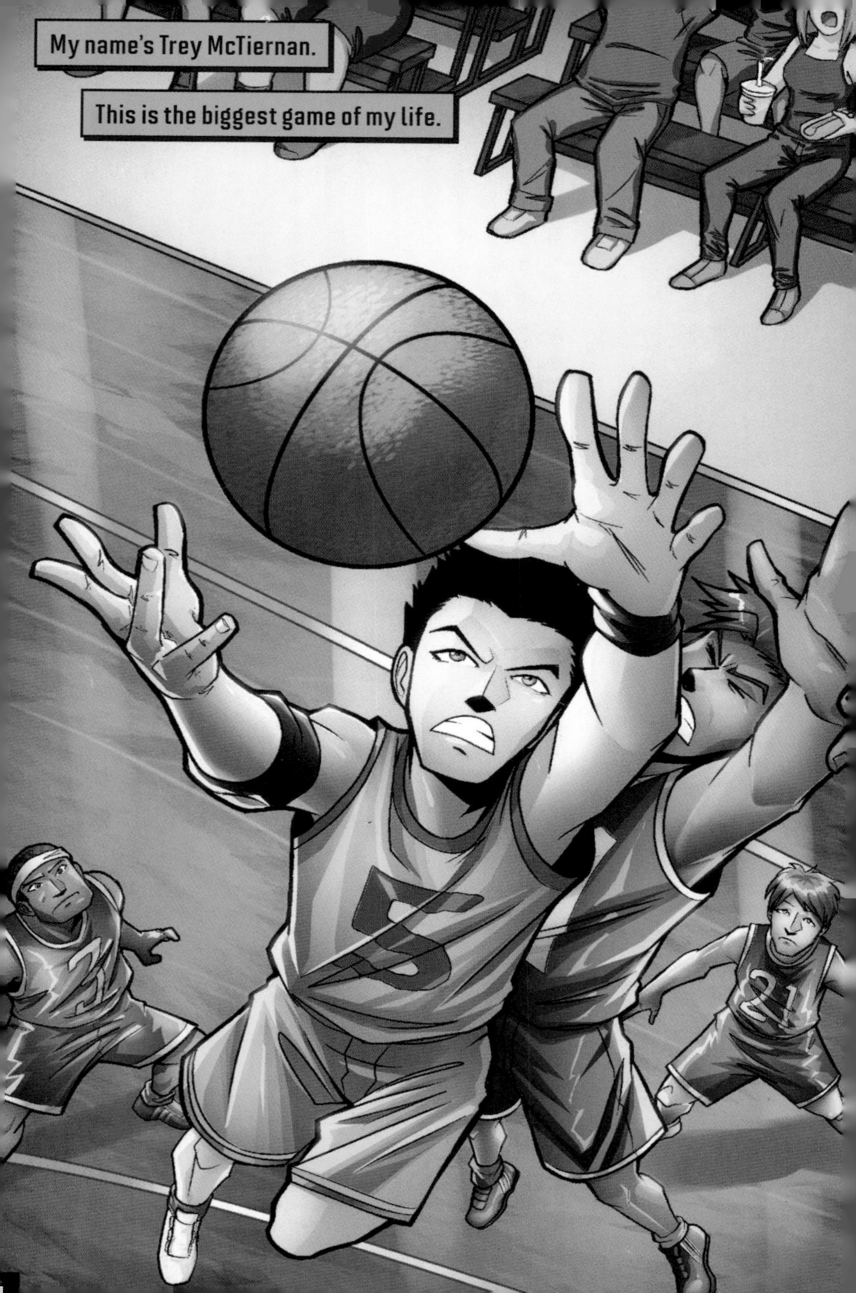
My name's Trey McTiernan.
This is the biggest game of my life.

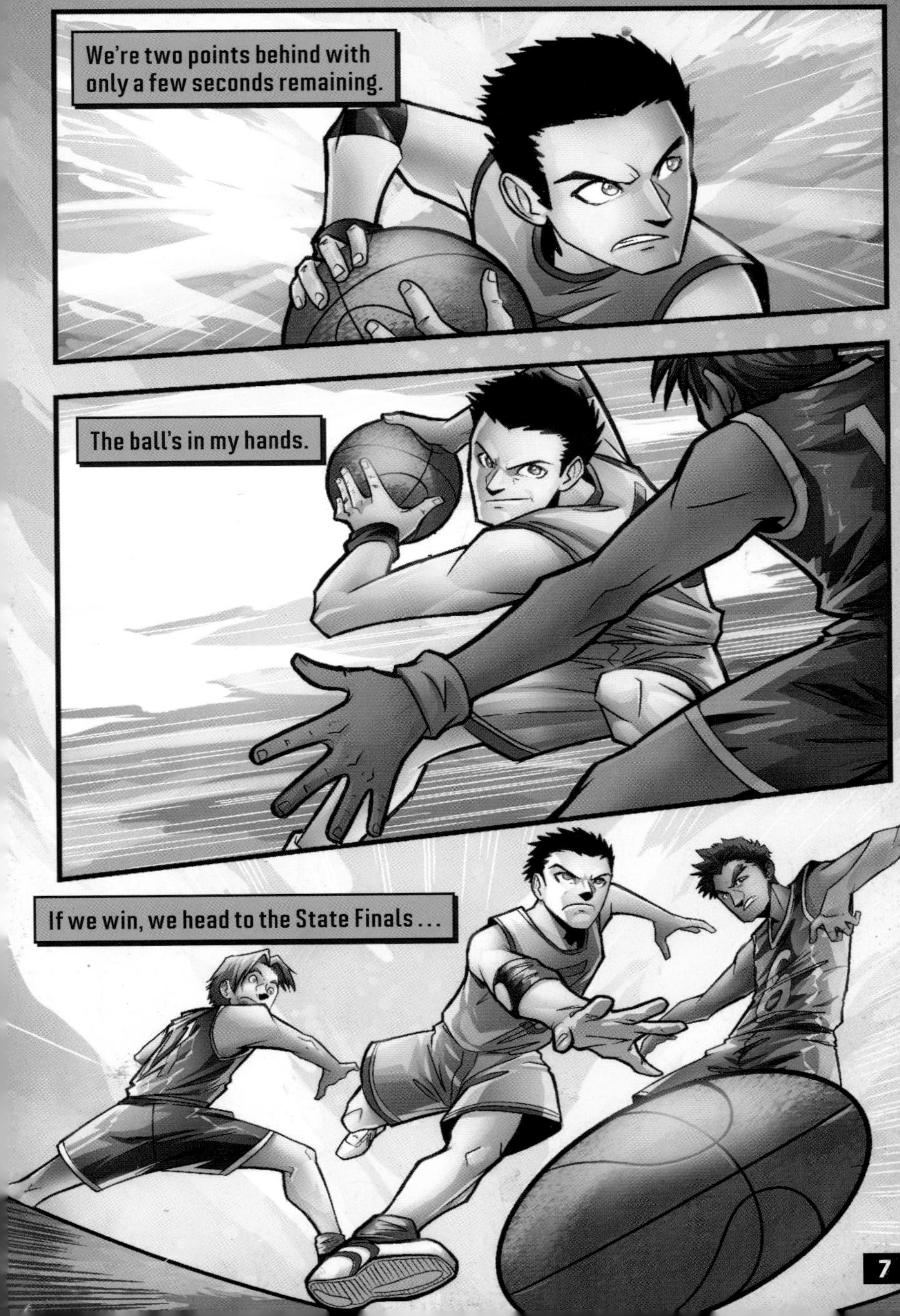

We're two points behind with only a few seconds remaining.
The ball's in my hands.
If we win, we head to the State Finals . . .

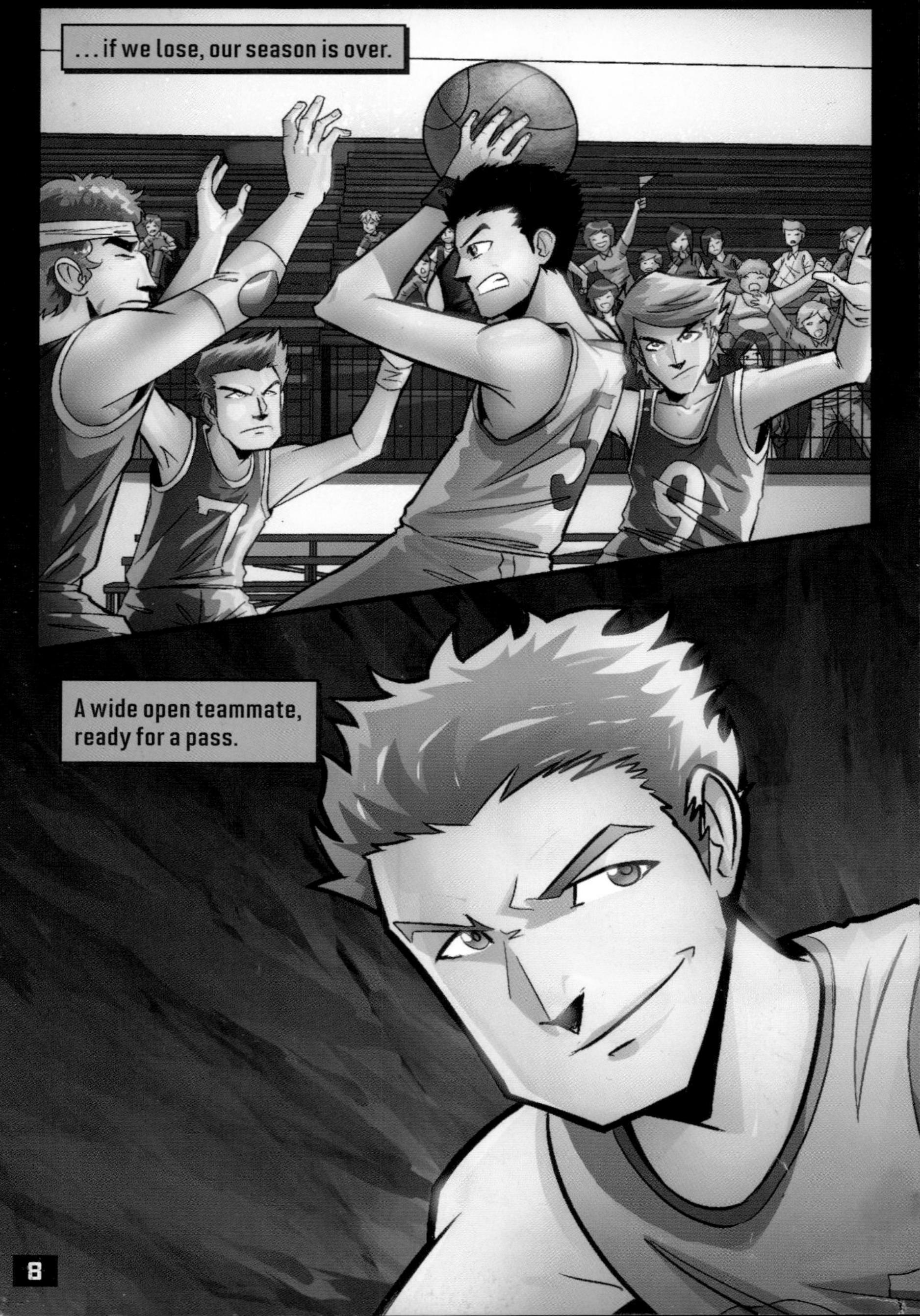
. . . if we lose, our season is over.
A wide open teammate, ready for a pass.

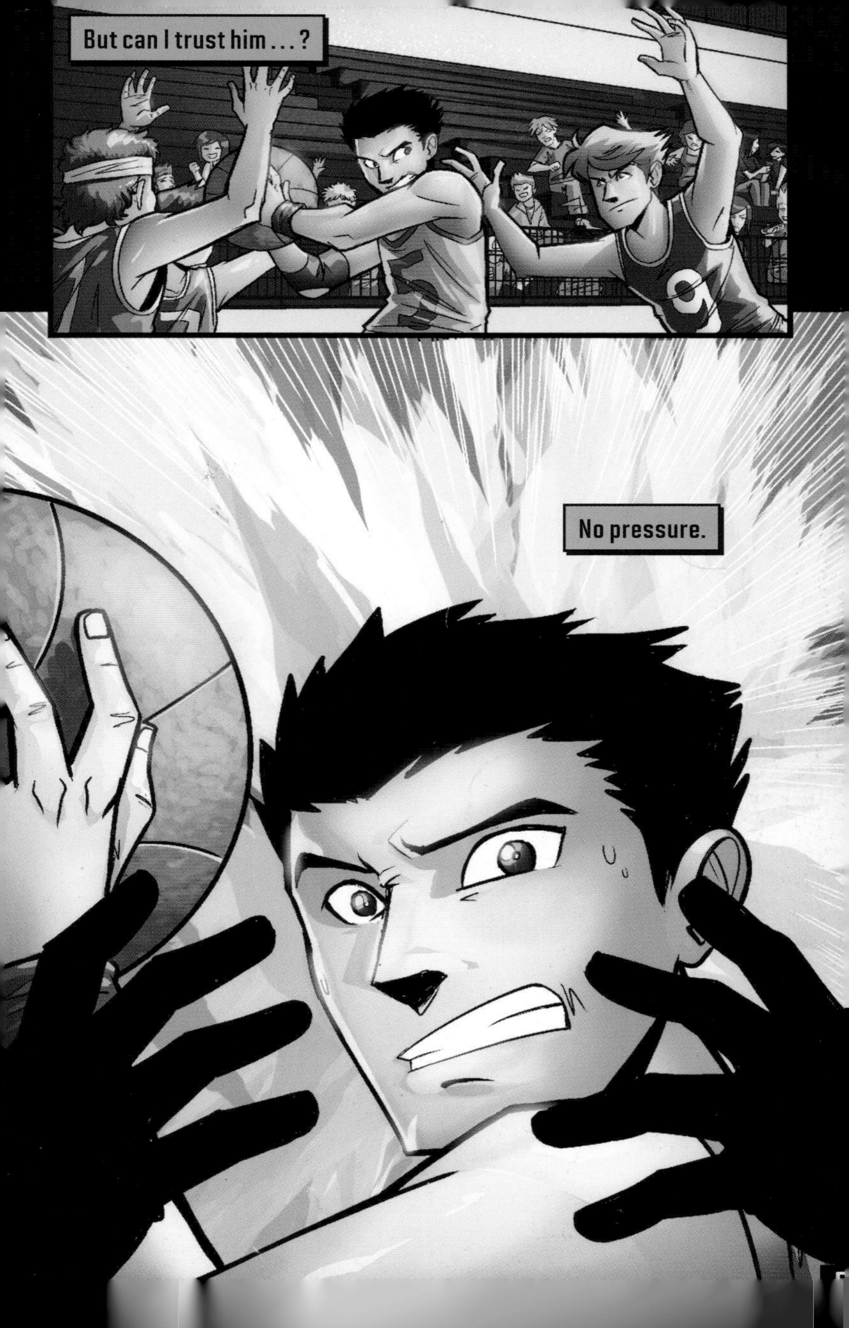
But can I trust him . . . ?
No pressure.

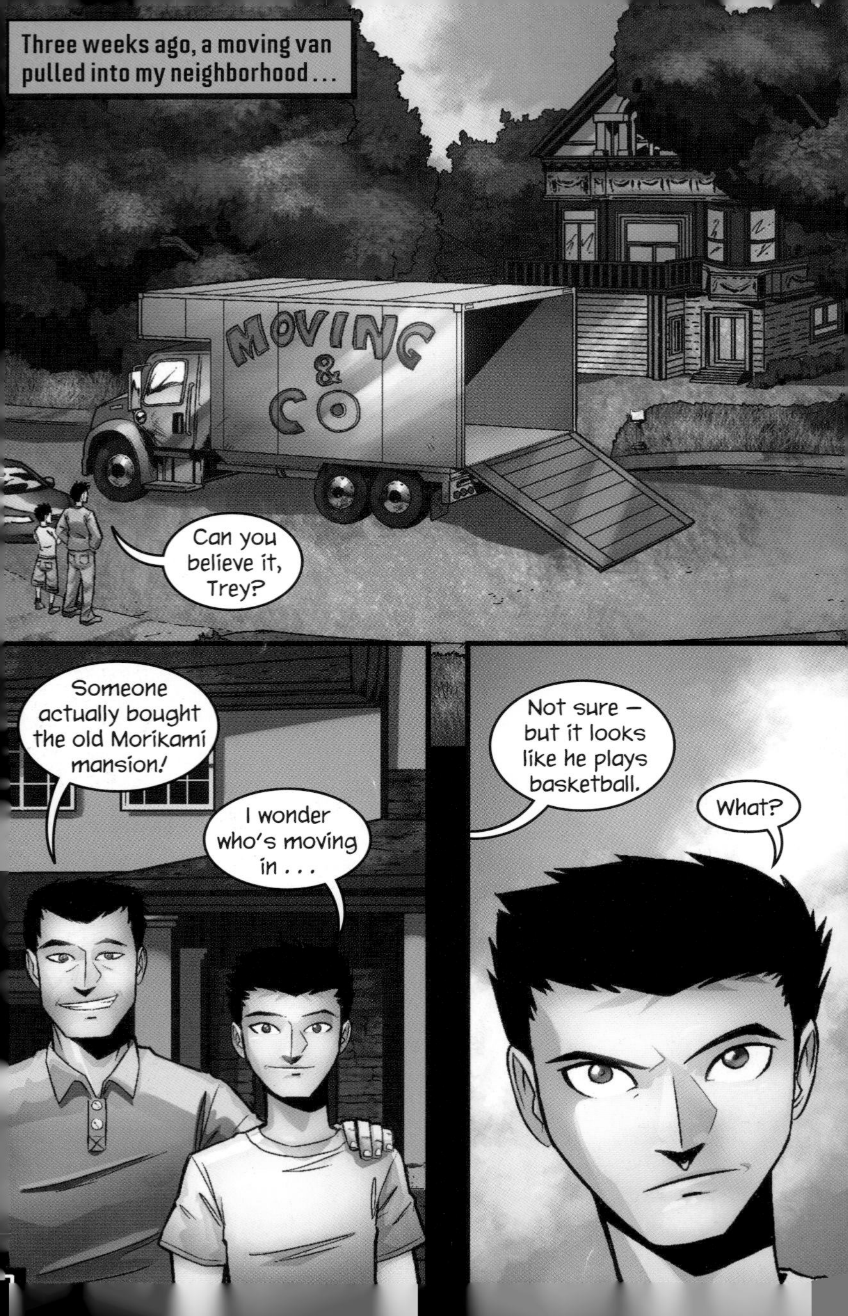

Three weeks ago, a moving van pulled into my neighborhood . . .
MOVING & CO
Can you believe it, Trey?
Someone actually bought the old Morikami mansion!
I wonder who's moving in . . .
Not sure — but it looks like he plays basketball.
What?

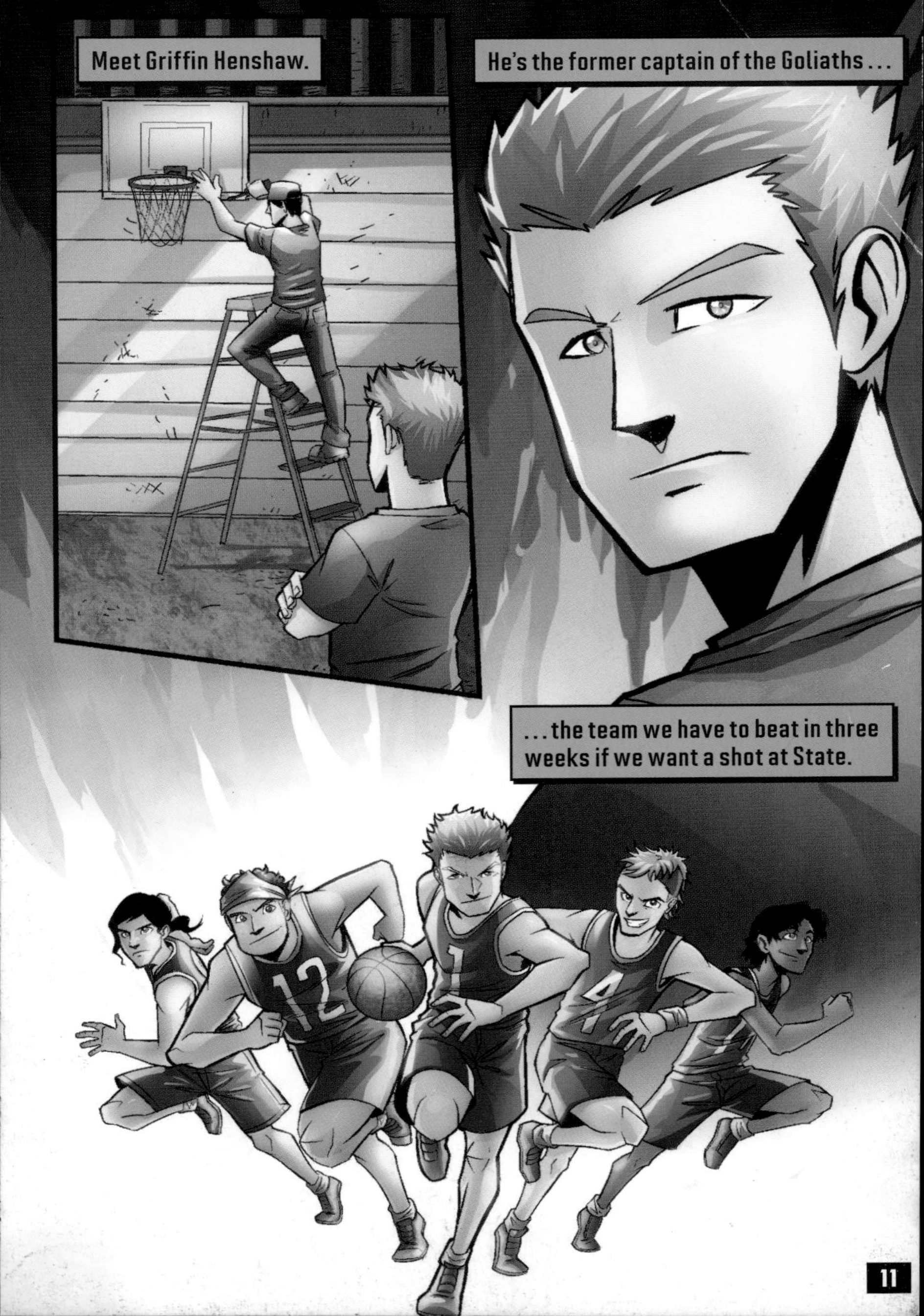
Meet Griffin Henshaw.
He's the former captain of the Goliaths . . .
. . . the team we have to beat in three weeks if we want a shot at State.

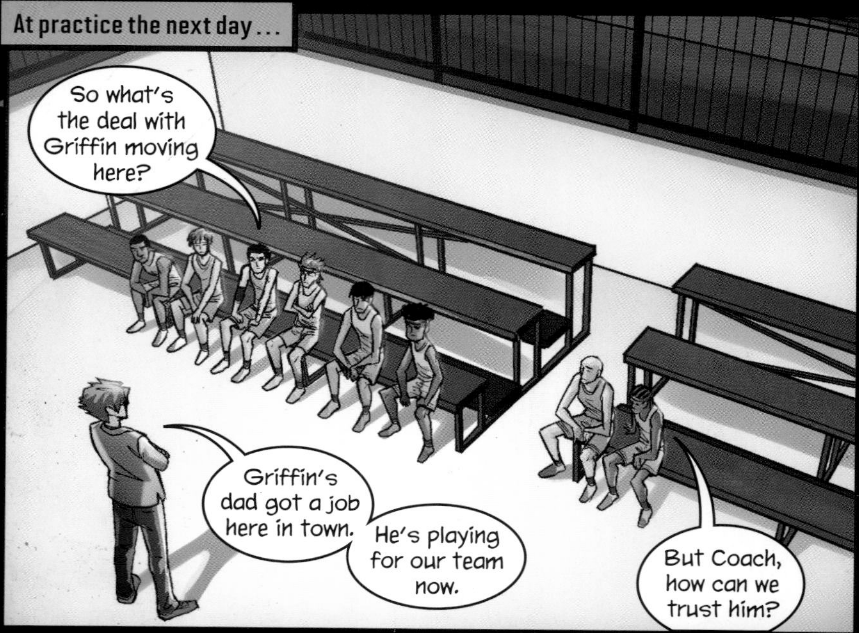
At practice the next day . . .
So what's the deal with Griffin moving here?
Griffin's dad got a job here in town.
He's playing for our team now.
But Coach, how can we trust him?

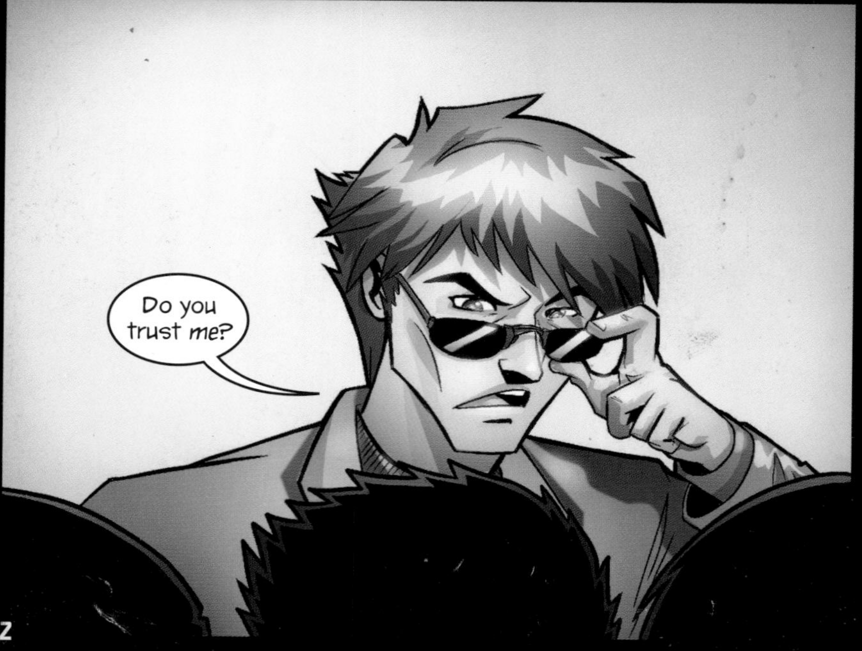
Do you trust *me*?

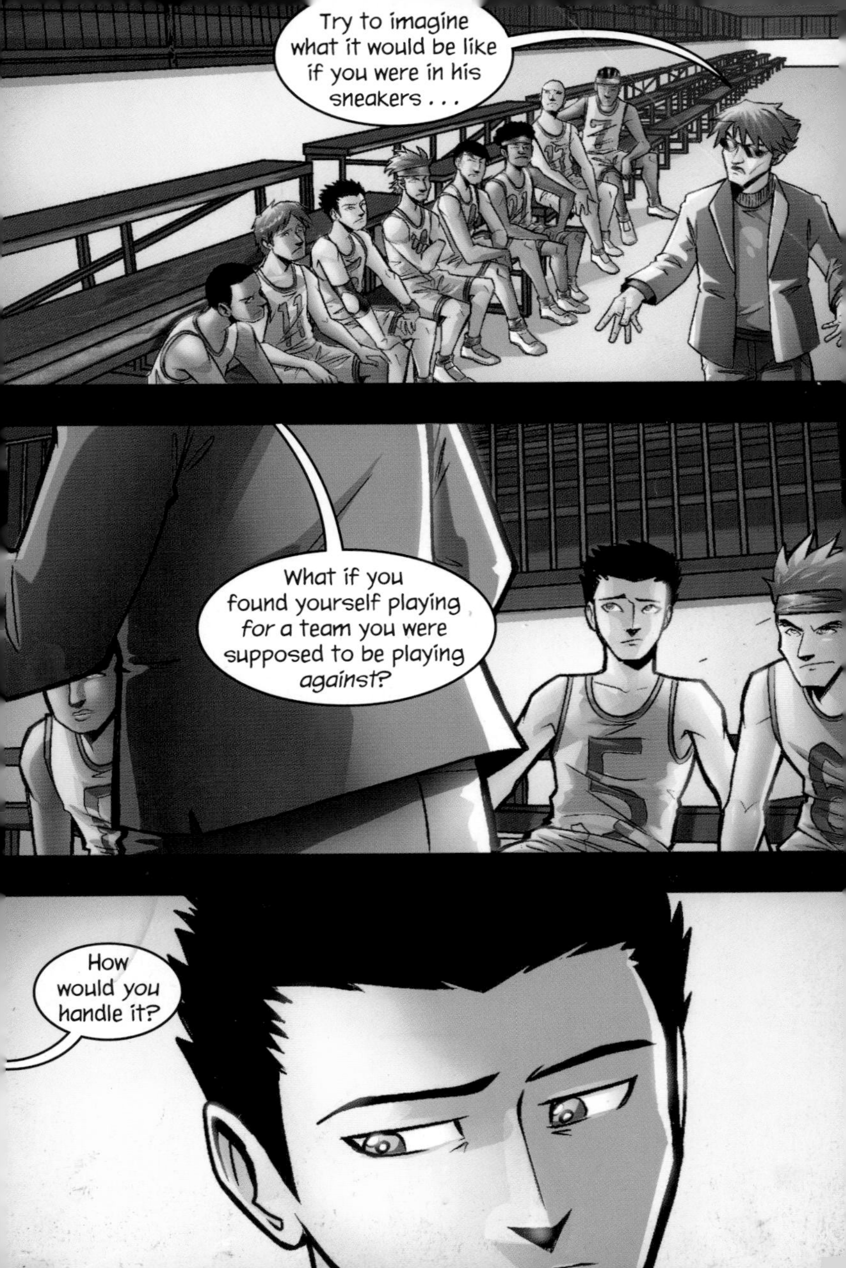
Try to imagine what it would be like if you were in his sneakers . . .
What if you found yourself playing *for* a team you were supposed to be playing *against*?
How would you handle it?

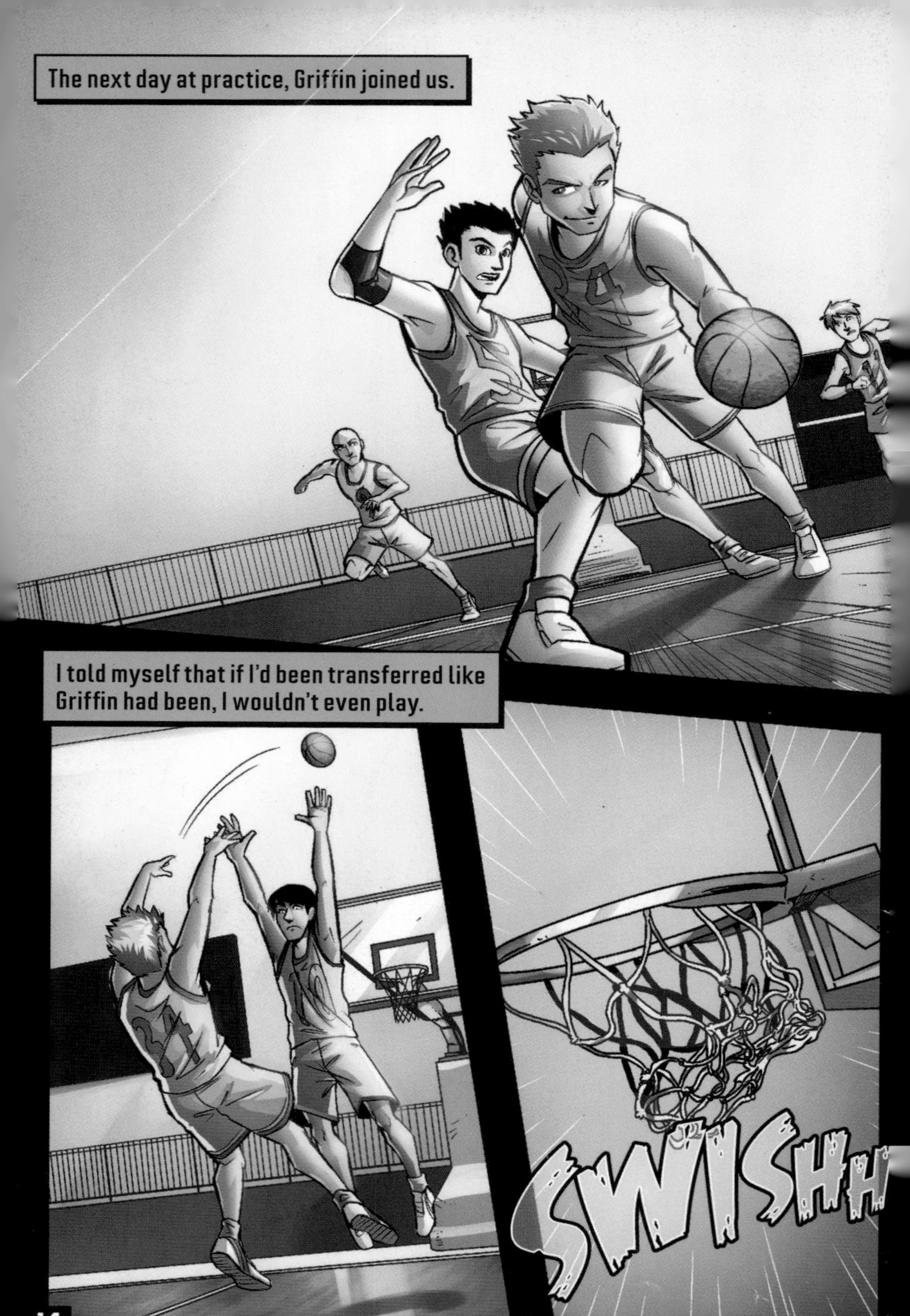
The next day at practice, Griffin joined us.
I told myself that if I'd been transferred like Griffin had been, I wouldn't even play.
SWISHH

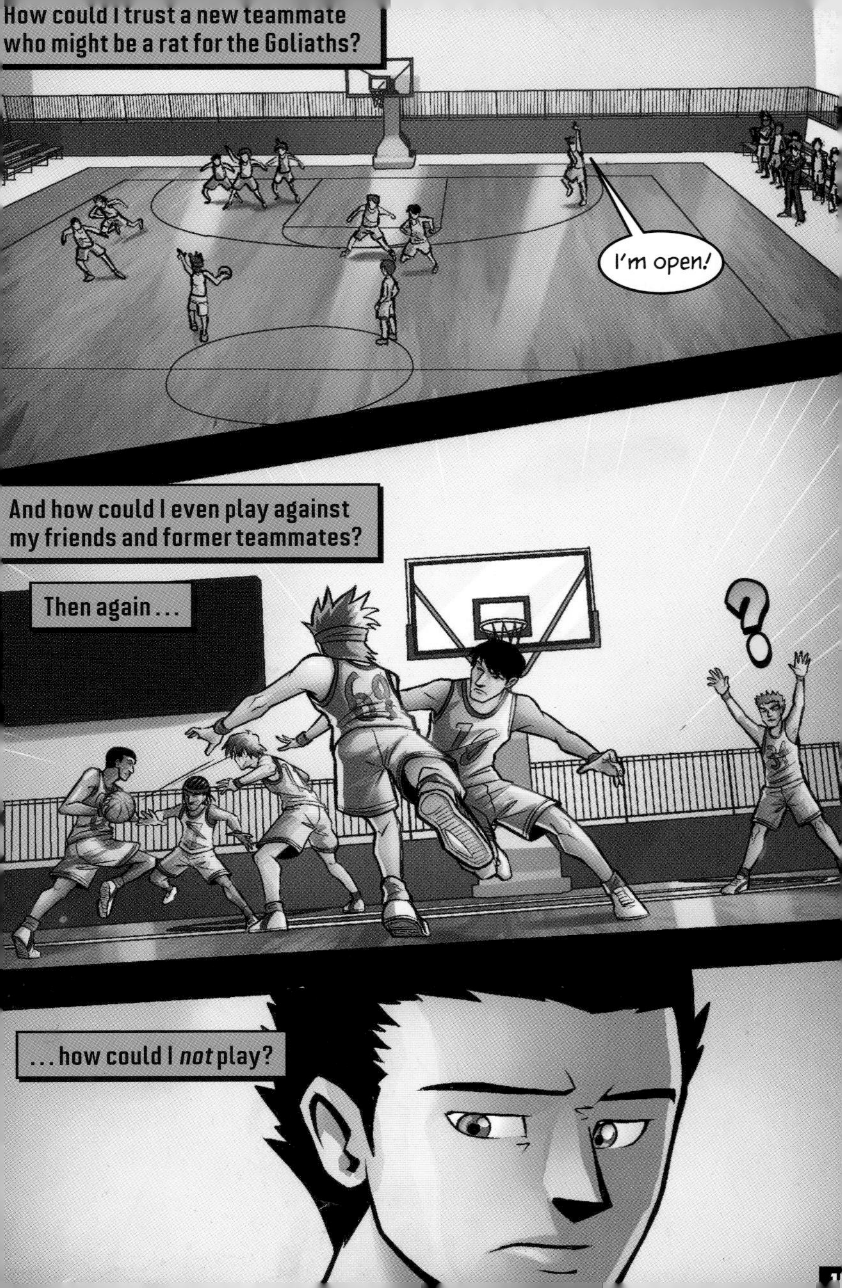
How could I trust a new teammate who might be a rat for the Goliaths?
I'm open!
And how could I even play against my friends and former teammates?
Then again . . .
?
. . . how could I *not* play?

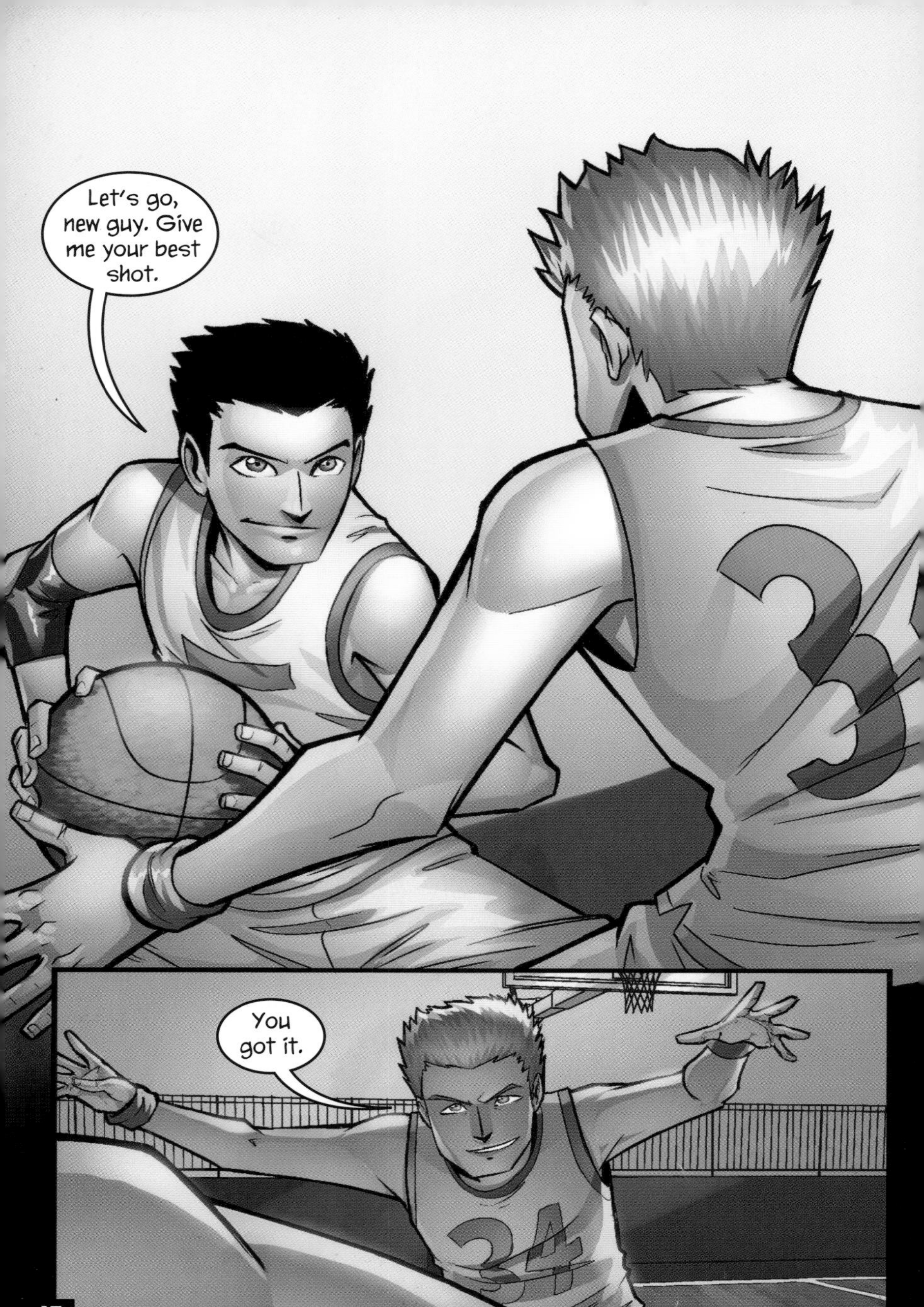
Let's go, new guy. Give me your best shot.
You got it.

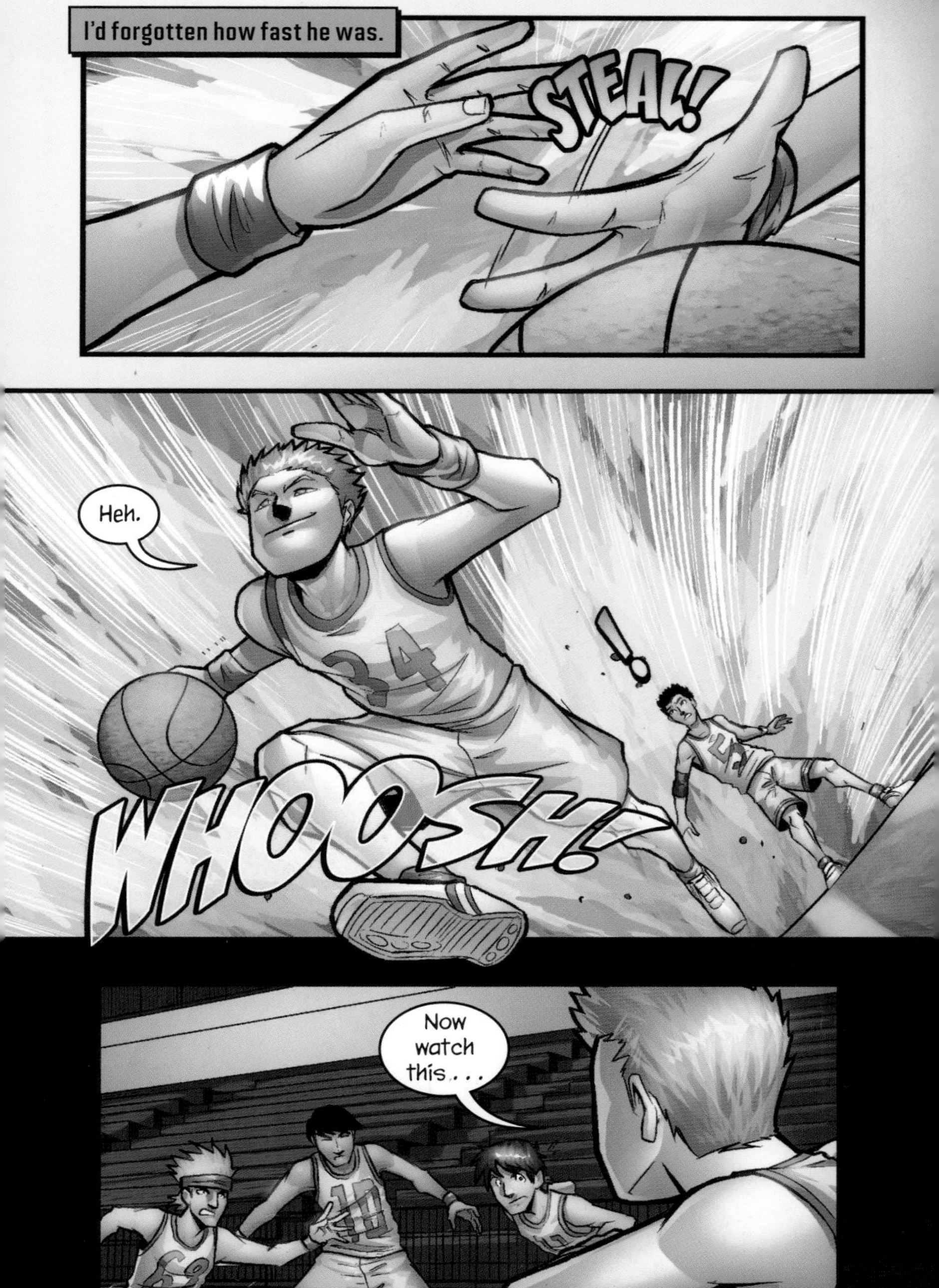
I'd forgotten how fast he was.
STEAL!
Heh.
!
WHOOSH!
Now watch this . . .

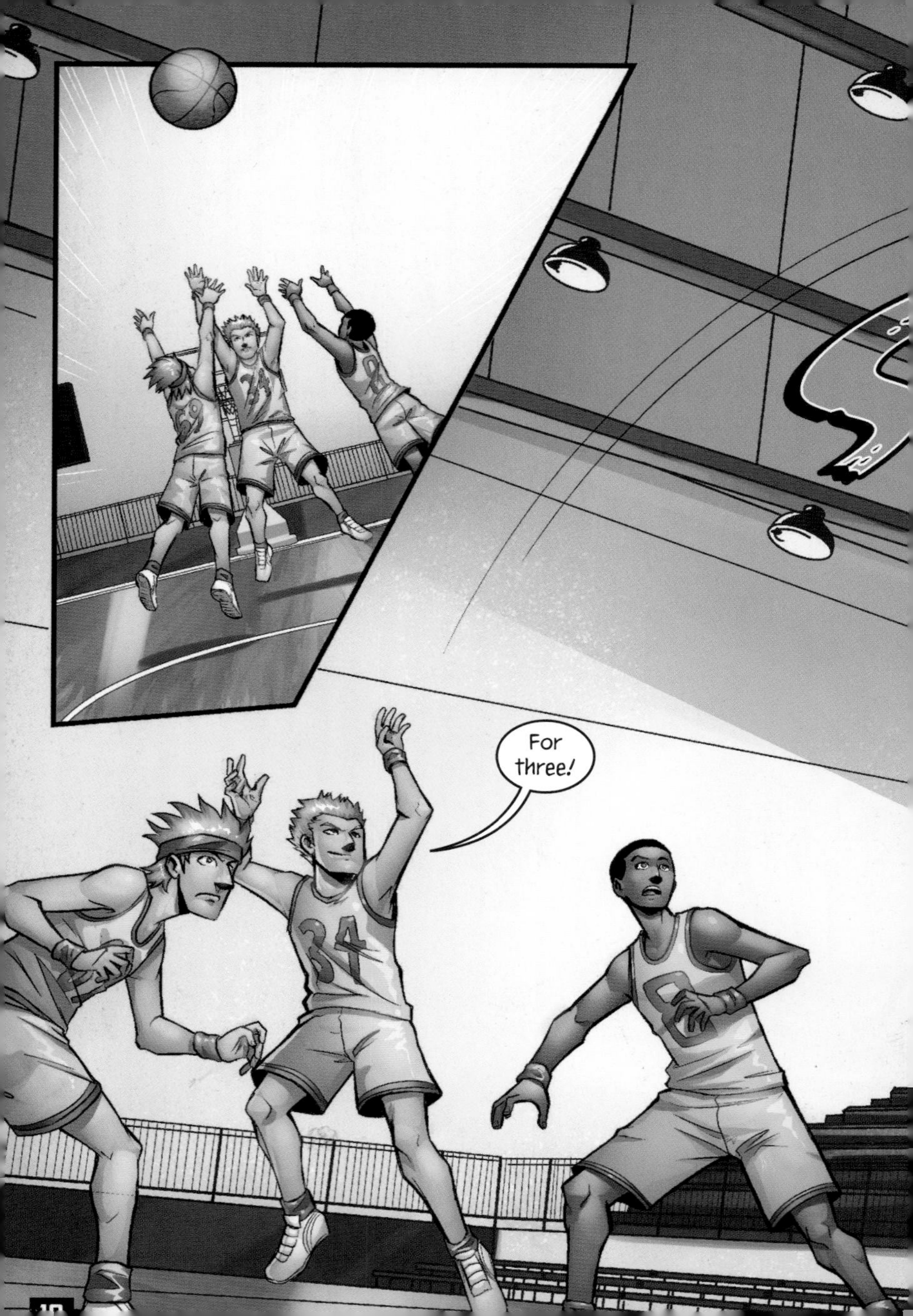
For three!

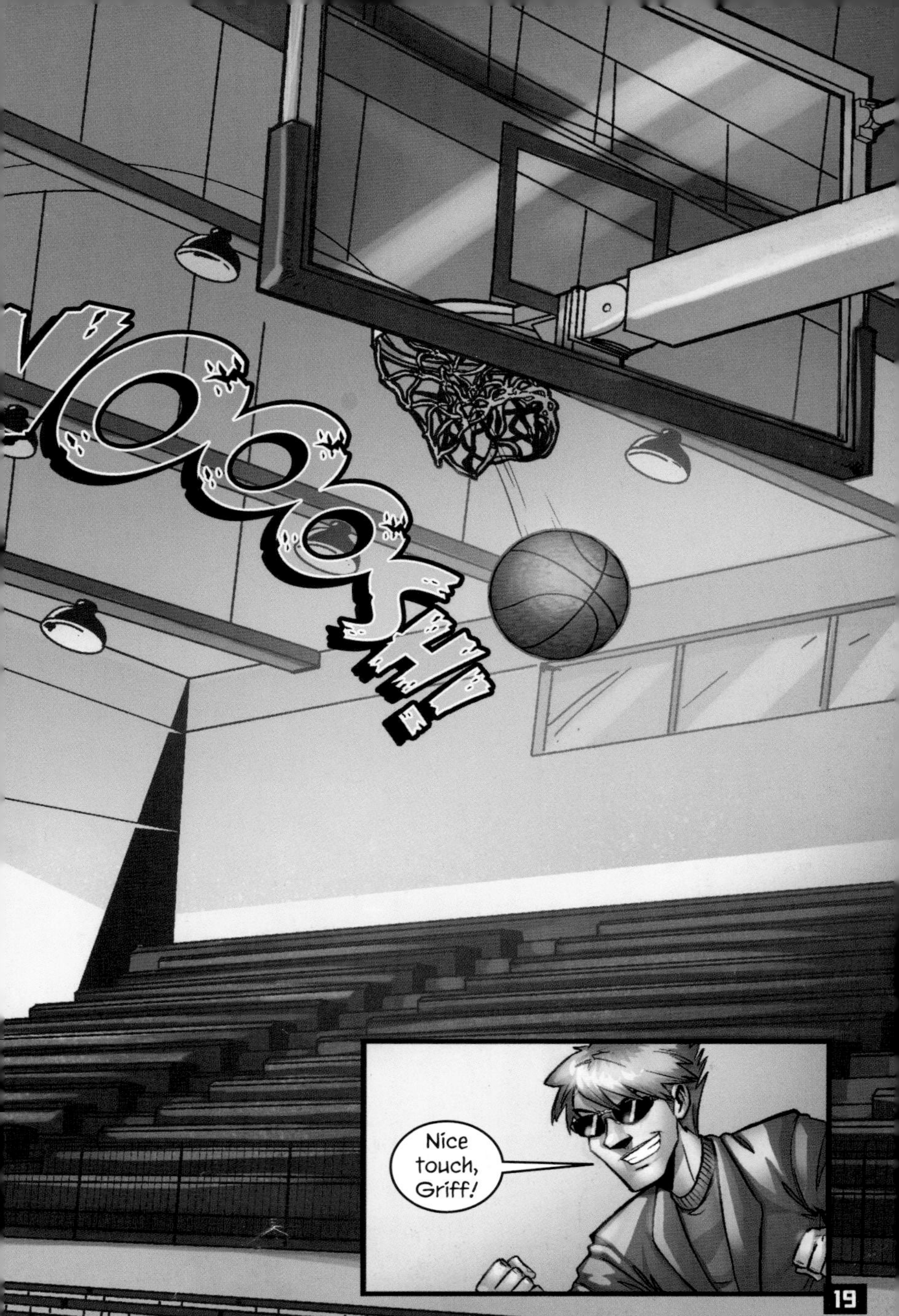
WOOOSH!!
Nice touch, Griff!

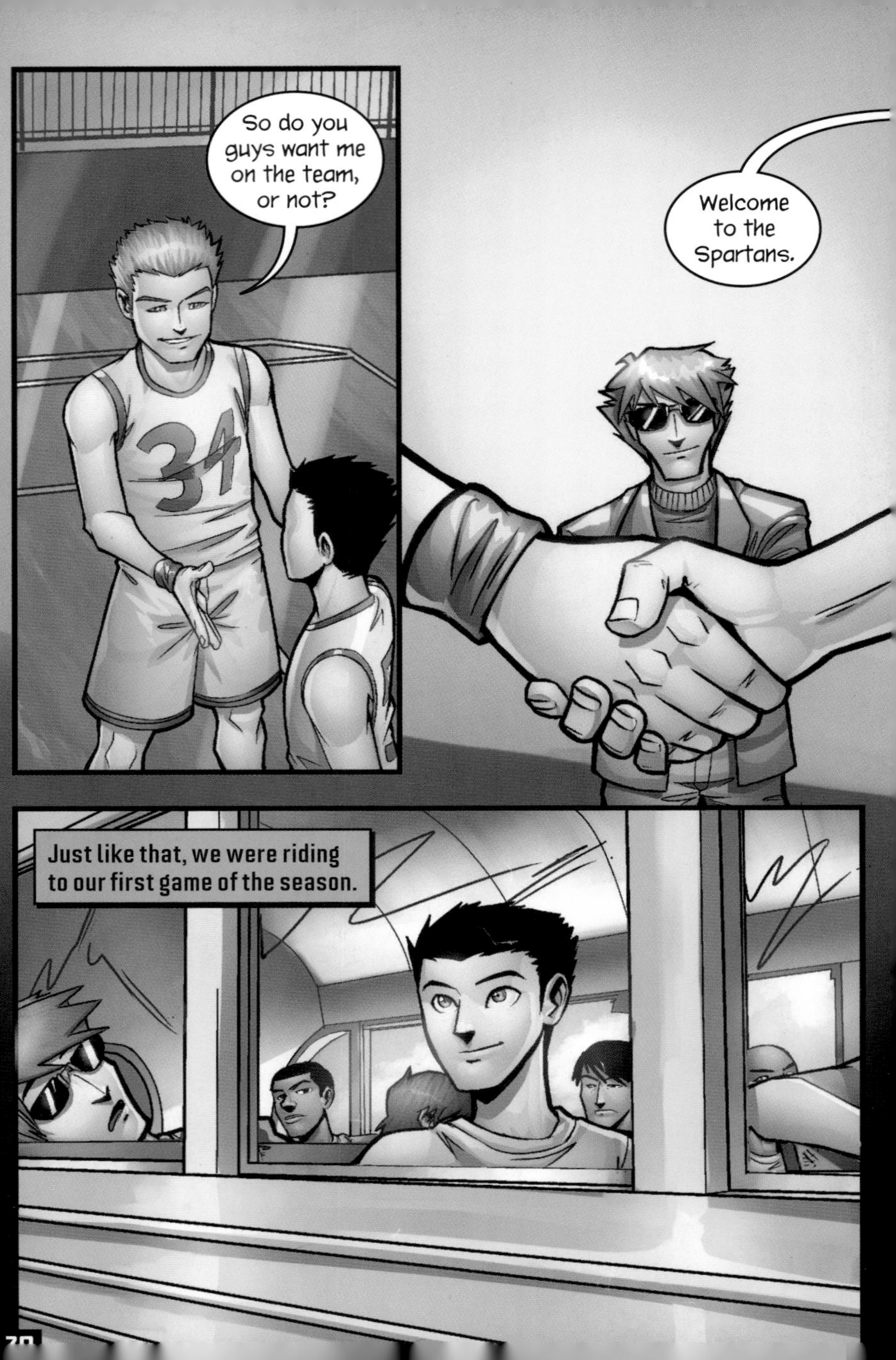
So do you guys want me on the team, or not?
Welcome to the Spartans.
Just like that, we were riding to our first game of the season.

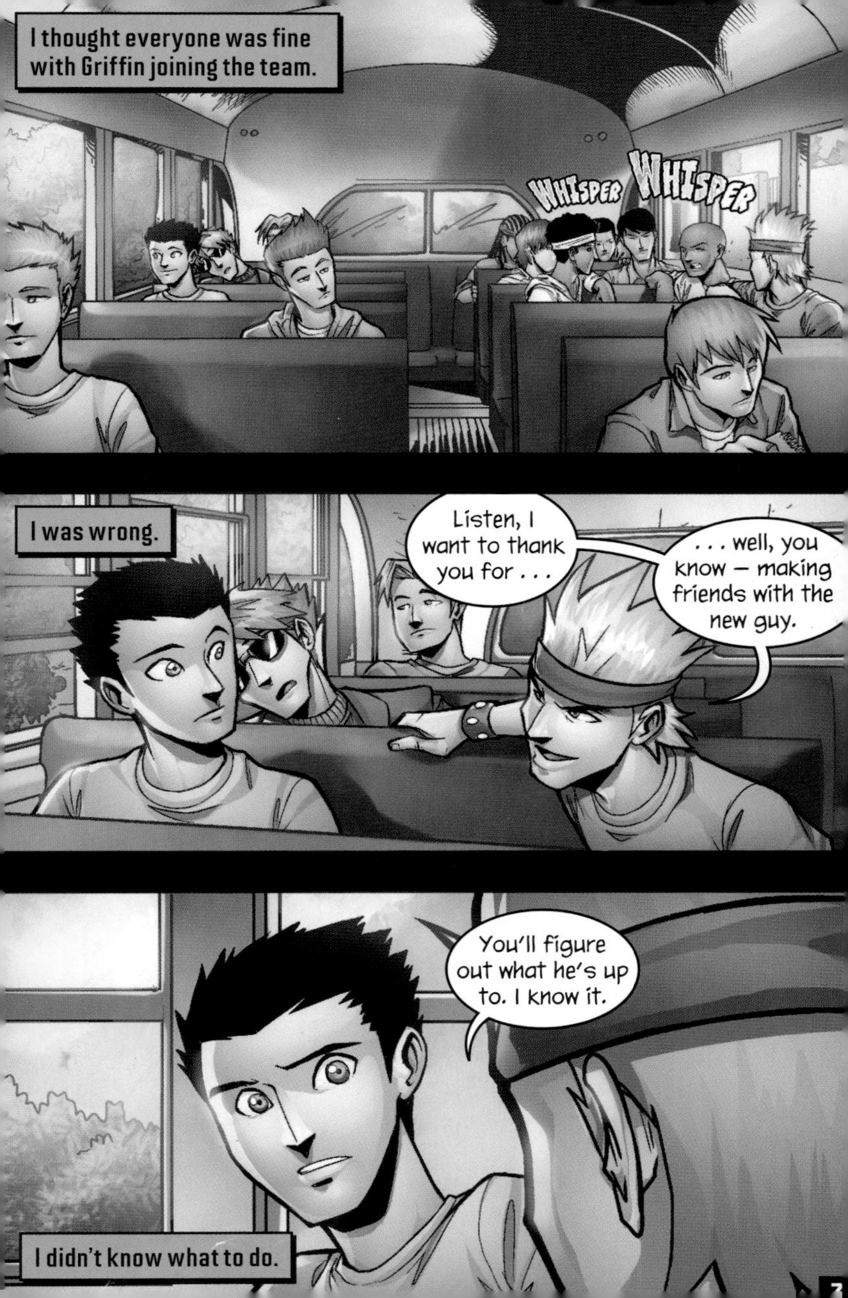

I thought everyone was fine with Griffin joining the team.
WHISPER WHISPER
I was wrong.
Listen, I want to thank you for . . .
. . . well, you know — making friends with the new guy.
You'll figure out what he's up to. I know it.
I didn't know what to do.

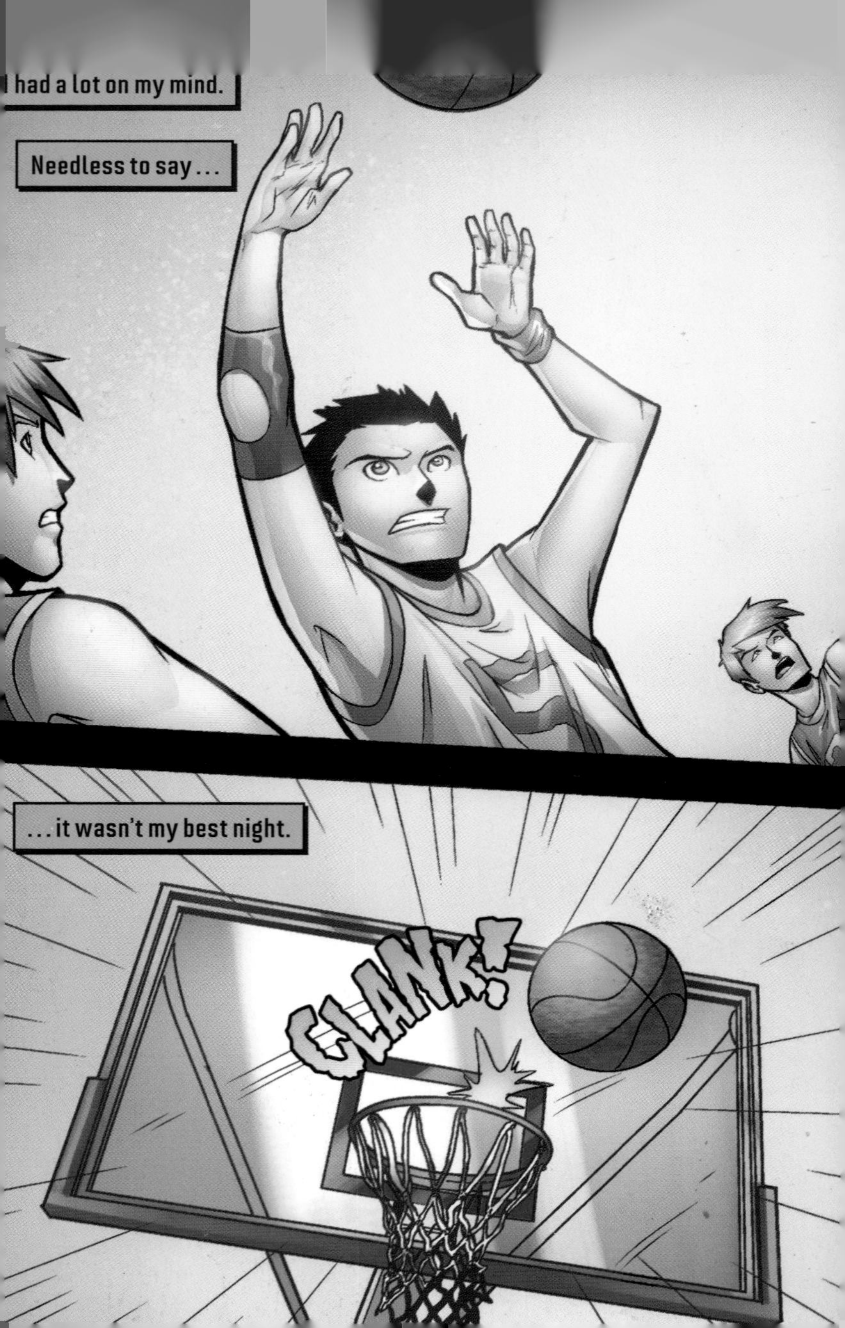
I had a lot on my mind.
Needless to say . . .
. . . it wasn't my best night.
CLANK!

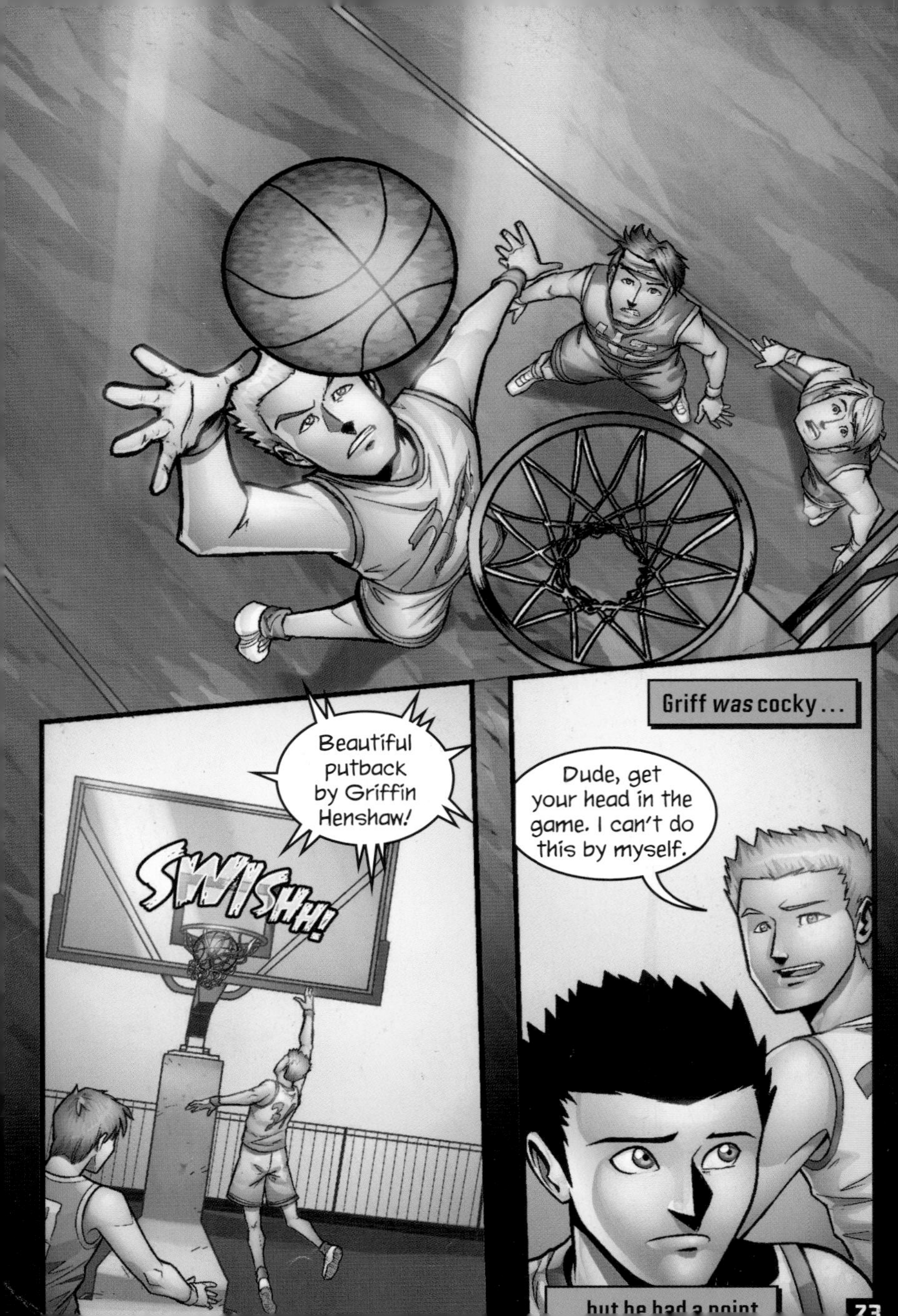
Beautiful putback by Griffin Henshaw!
SWISHH!
Griff *was* cocky . . .
Dude, get your head in the game. I can't do this by myself.
but he had a point

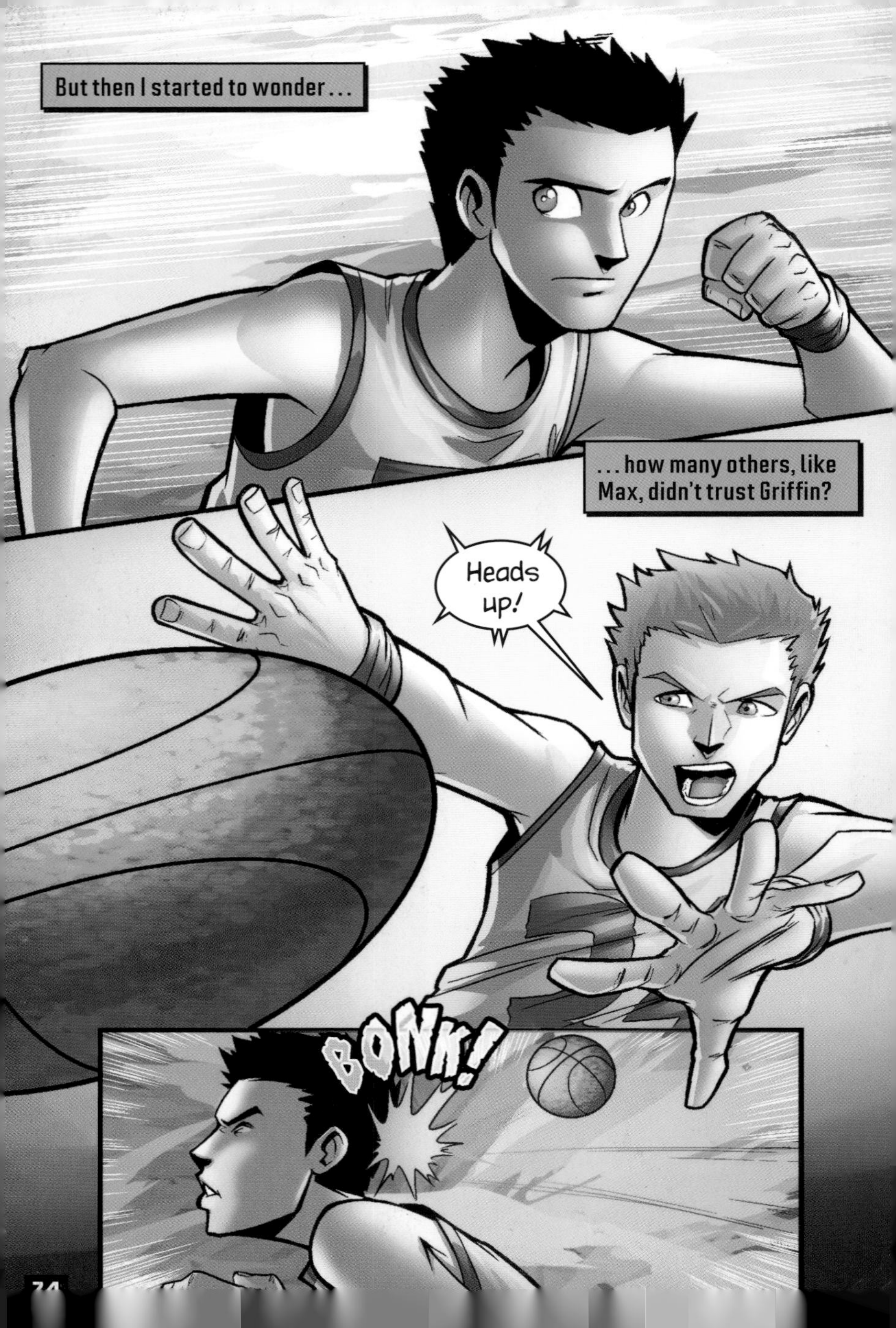
But then I started to wonder . . .
. . . how many others, like Max, didn't trust Griffin?
Heads up!
BONK!

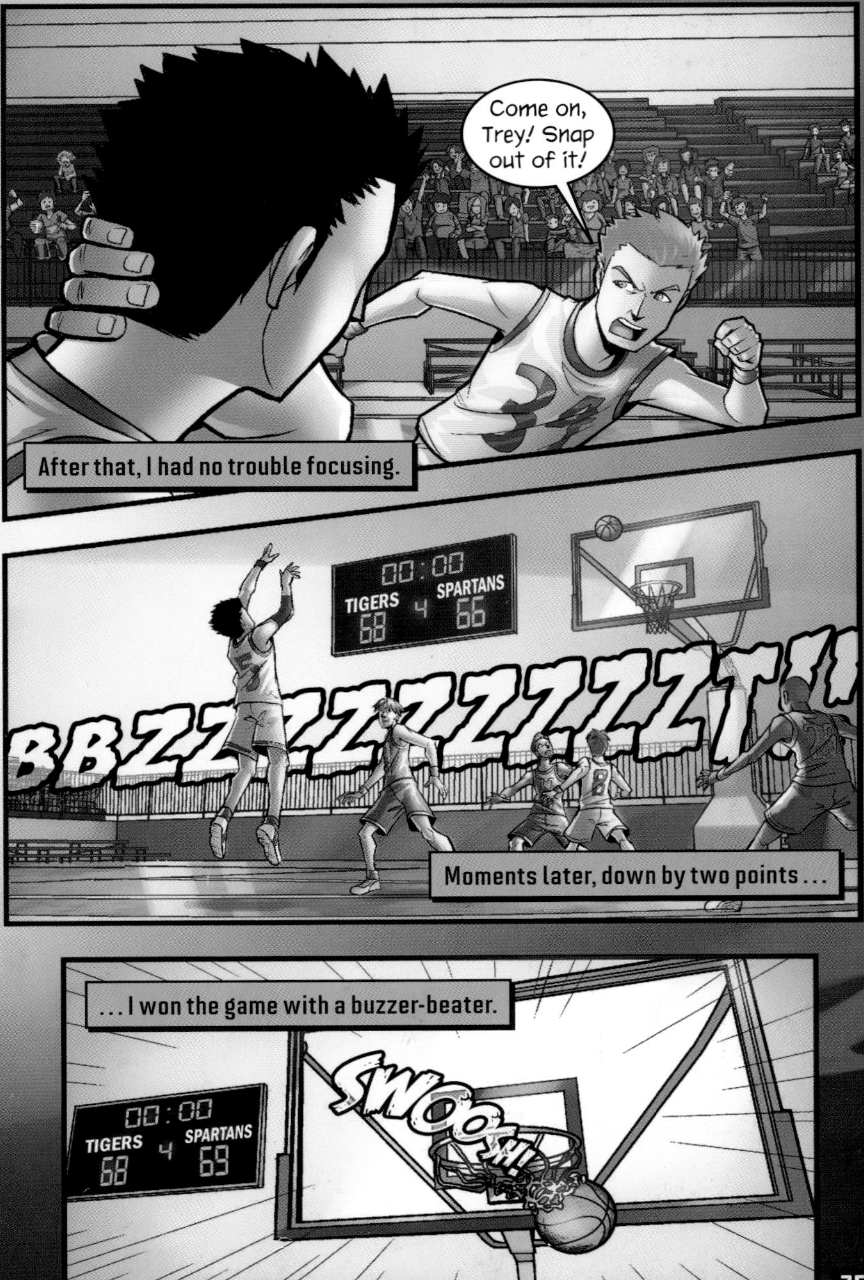
Come on, Trey! Snap out of it!
After that, I had no trouble focusing.
00:00
TIGERS 4 SPARTANS
68 66
BBZZZZZZZZZZT!!
Moments later, down by two points . . .
. . . I won the game with a buzzer-beater.
00:00
TIGERS 4 SPARTANS
68 69
SWOOSH!

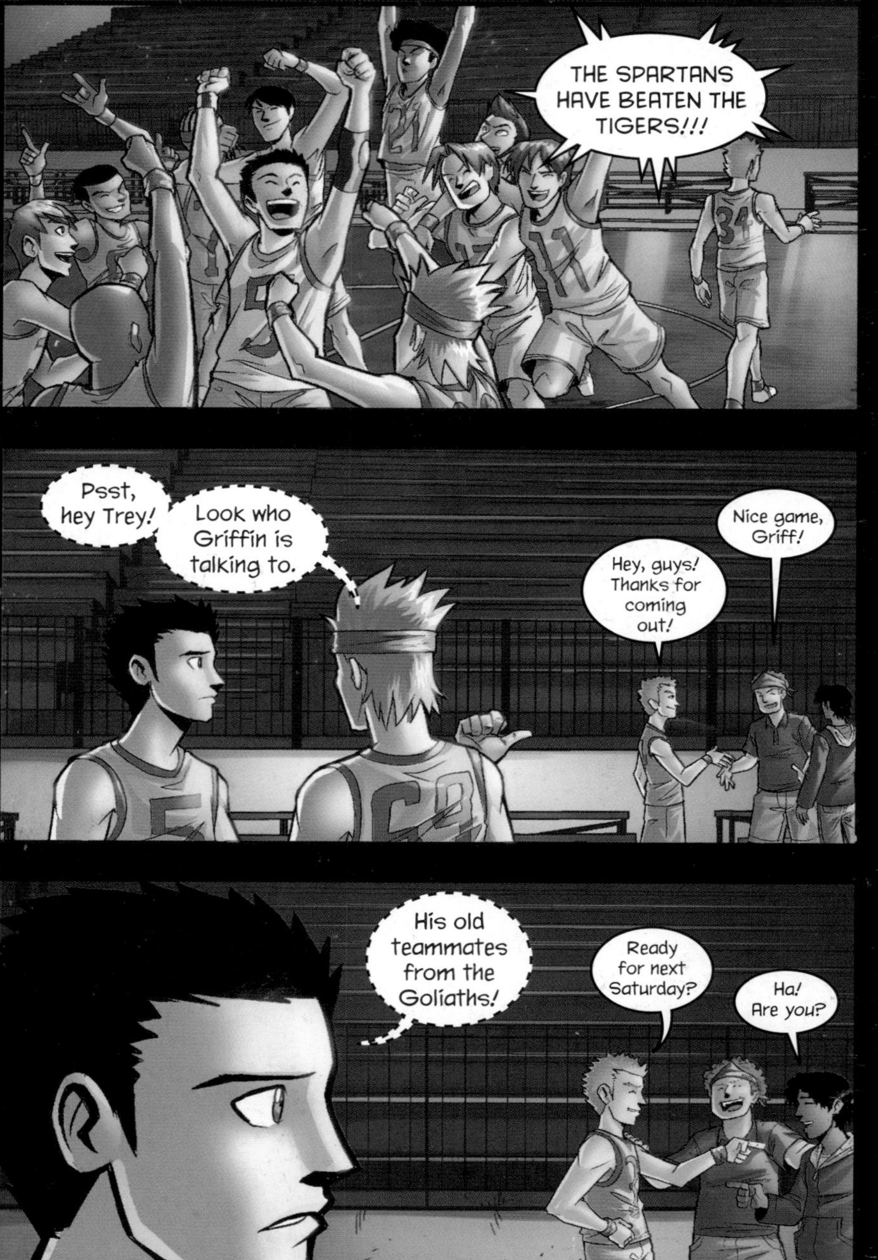
THE SPARTANS HAVE BEATEN THE TIGERS!!!
Psst, hey Trey!
Look who Griffin is talking to.
Hey, guys! Thanks for coming out!
Nice game, Griff!
His old teammates from the Goliaths!
Ready for next Saturday?
Ha! Are you?

I bet he's telling them our weak spots, how our plays work — everything.

Maybe he's just hanging out with his friends, Max . . .

Don't be stupid. He's a rat, and you know it.

What if Max was right?

Let's go grab some pizza.

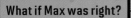

Great idea!

I decided to find out for myself.

27

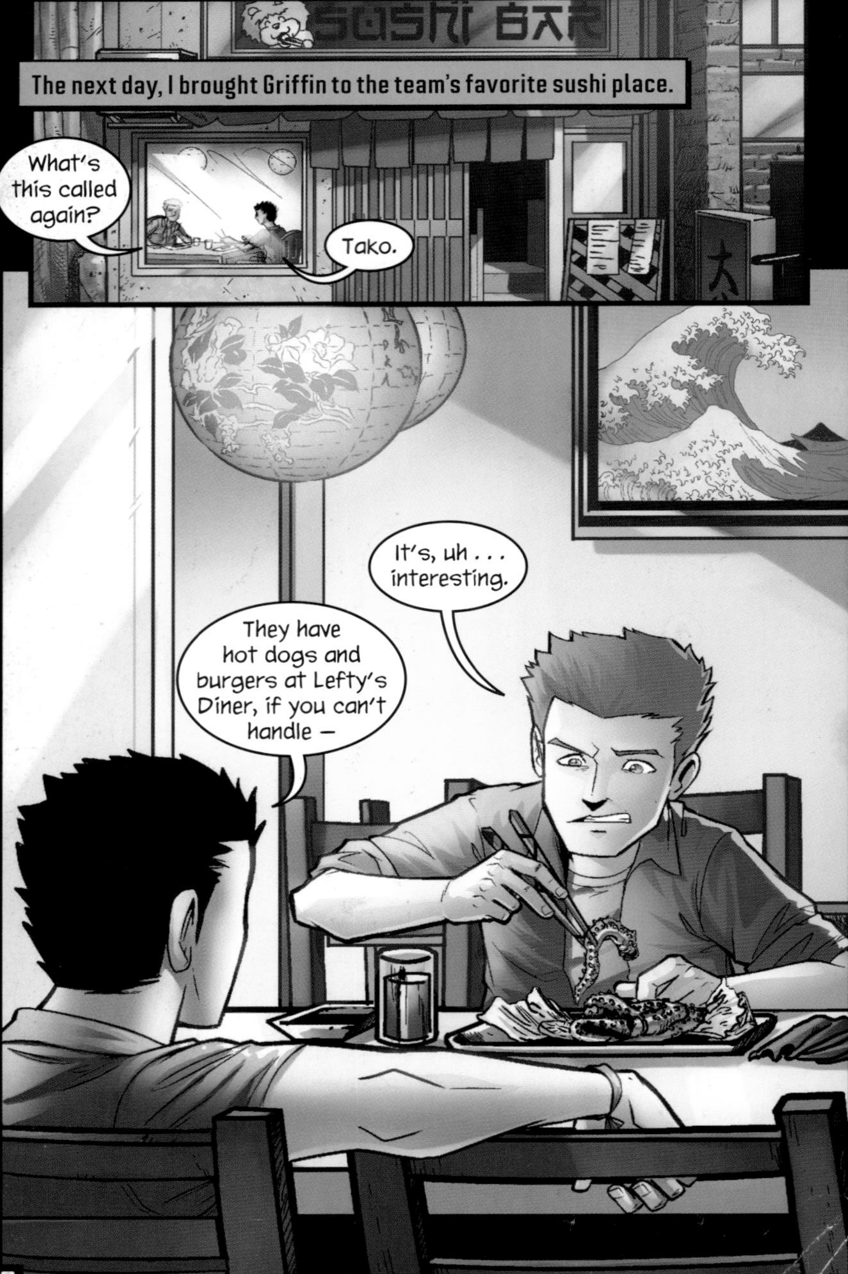
SUSHI BAR
The next day, I brought Griffin to the team's favorite sushi place.
What's this called again?
Tako.
It's, uh . . . interesting.
They have hot dogs and burgers at Lefty's Diner, if you can't handle –

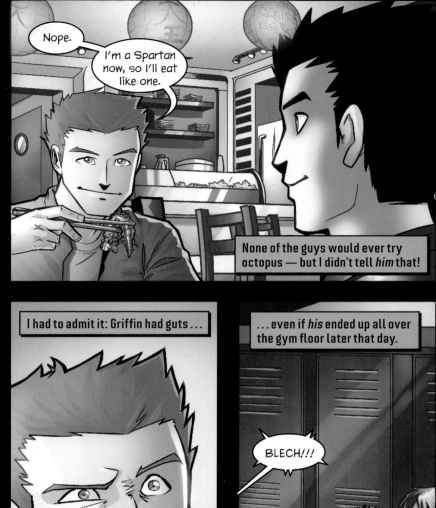

Nope. I'm a Spartan now, so I'll eat like one.

None of the guys would ever try octopus — but I didn't tell *him* that!

I had to admit it: Griffin had guts...

...even if *his* ended up all over the gym floor later that day.

BLECH!!!

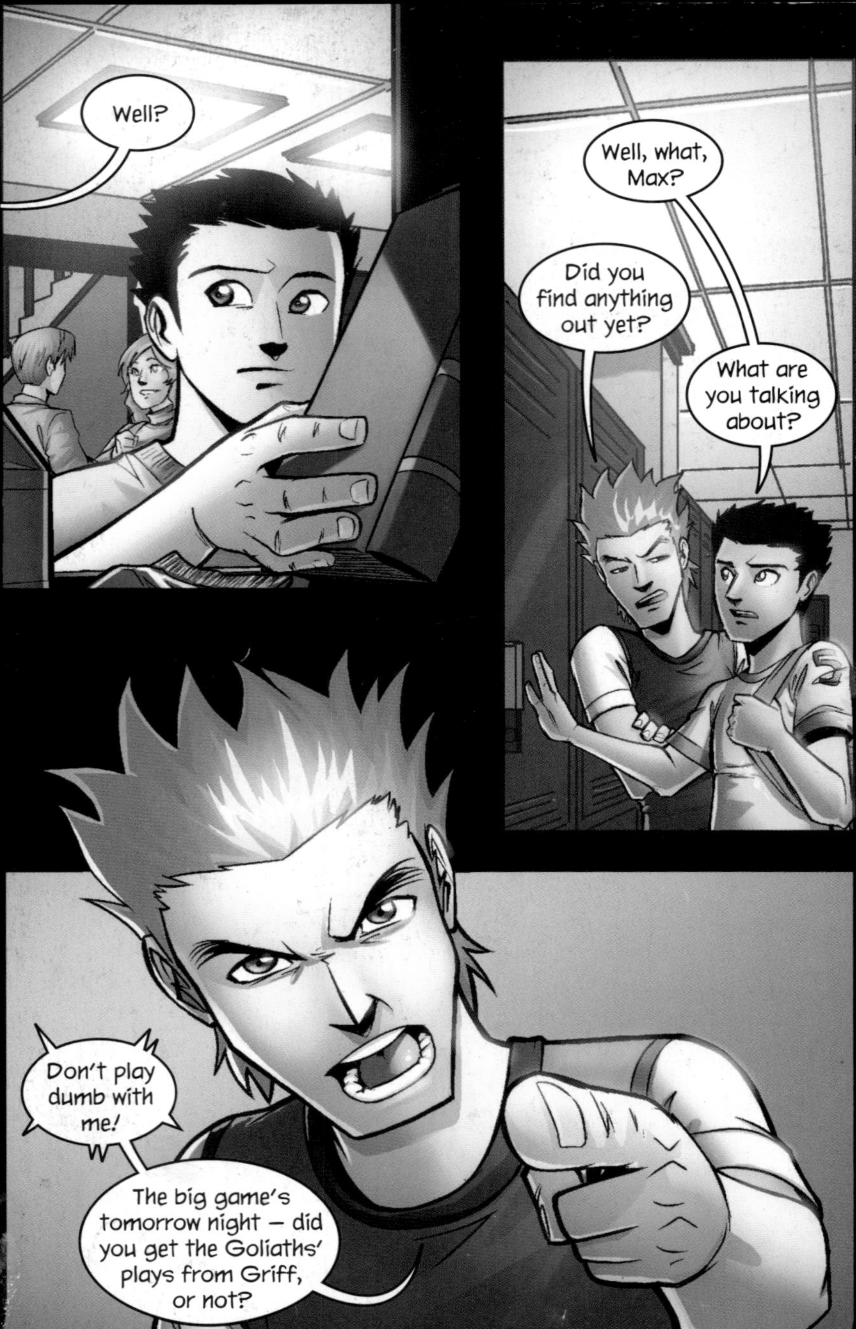
Well?
Well, what, Max?
Did you find anything out yet?
What are you talking about?
Don't play dumb with me!
The big game's tomorrow night — did you get the Goliaths' plays from Griff, or not?

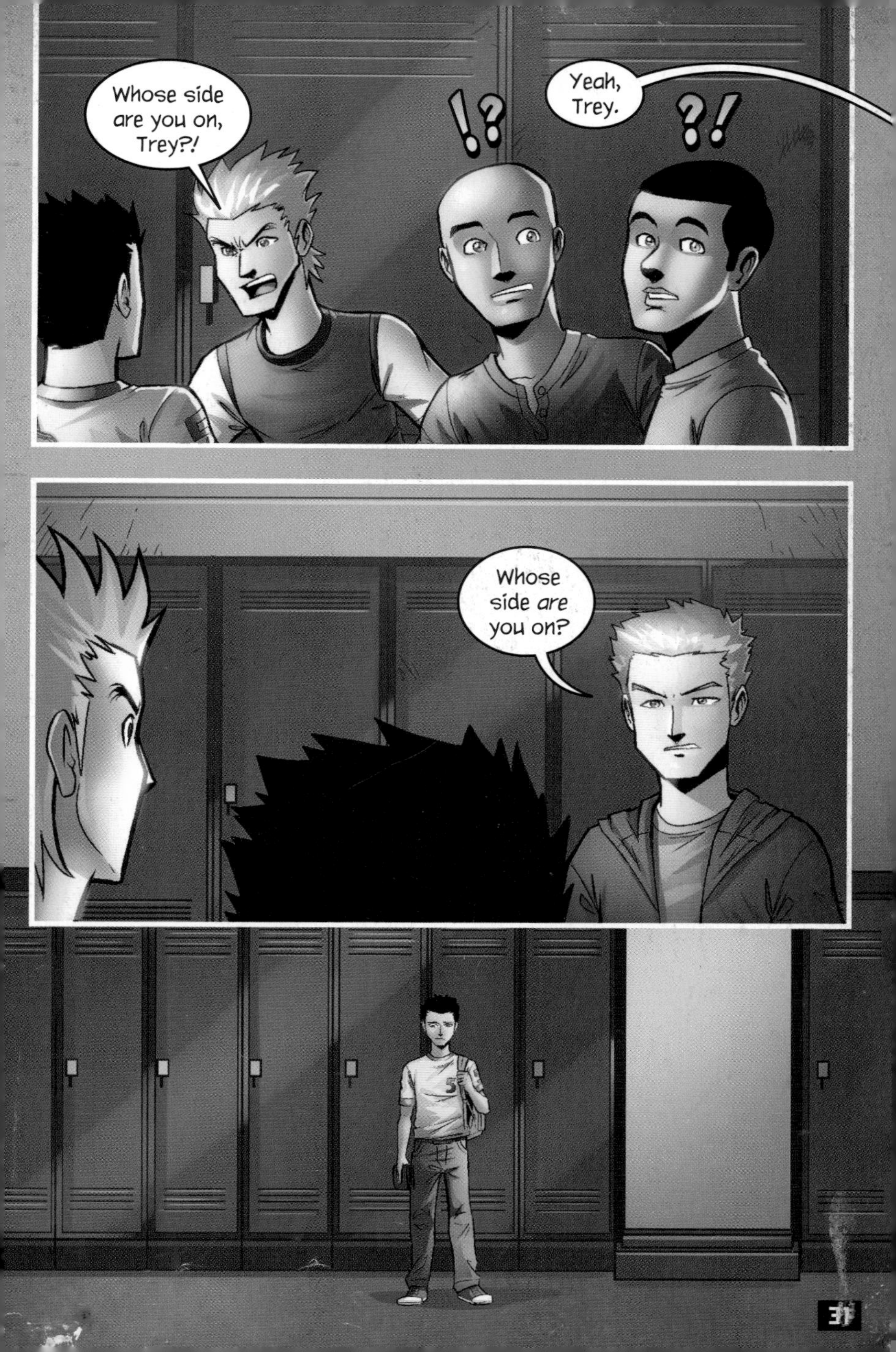
Whose side are you on, Trey?!
!?
Yeah, Trey.
?!
Whose side *are* you on?

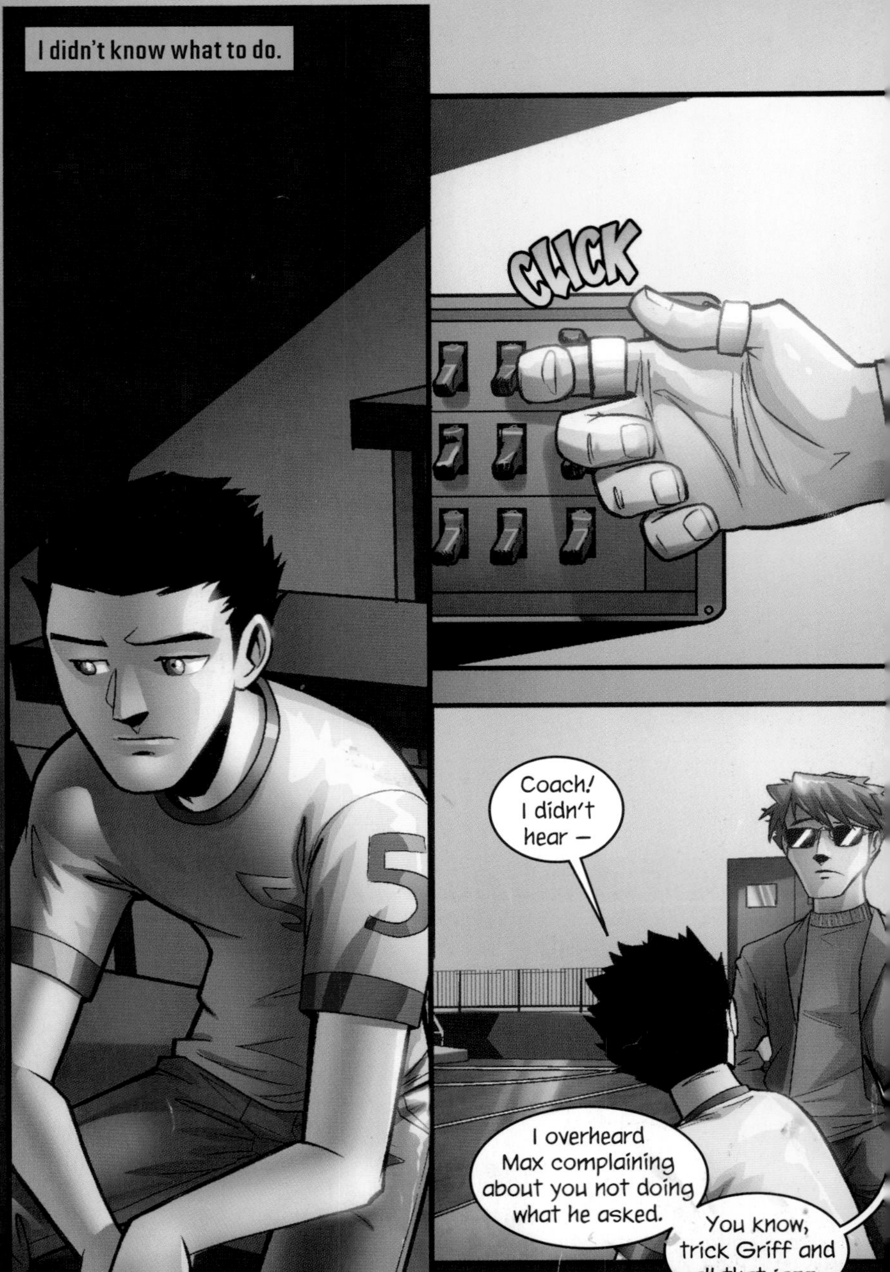

I didn't know what to do.
CLICK
Coach! I didn't hear —
I overheard Max complaining about you not doing what he asked.
You know, trick Griff and all that jazz.

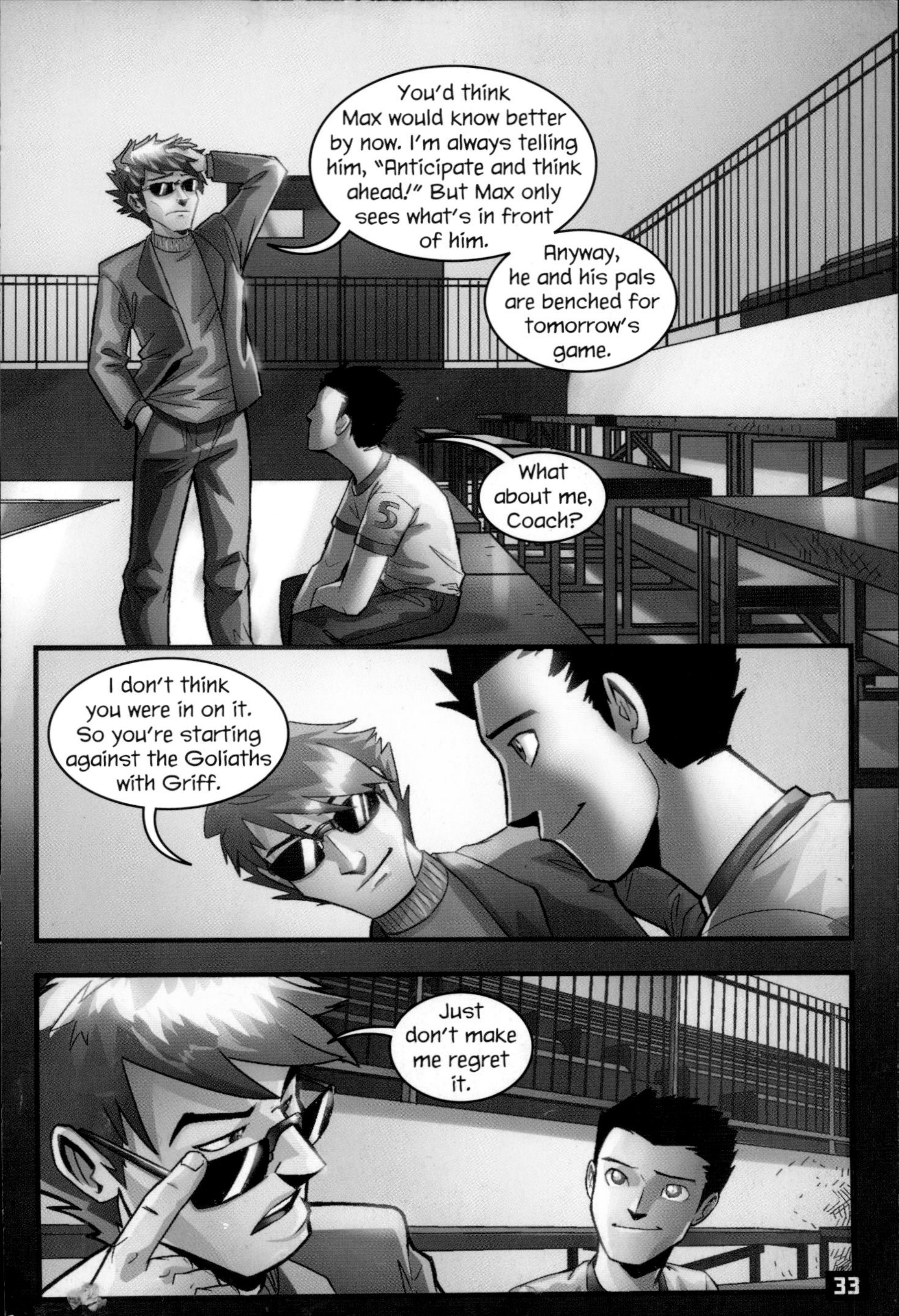
You'd think Max would know better by now. I'm always telling him, "Anticipate and think ahead!" But Max only sees what's in front of him.
Anyway, he and his pals are benched for tomorrow's game.
What about me, Coach?
I don't think you were in on it. So you're starting against the Goliaths with Griff.
Just don't make me regret it.

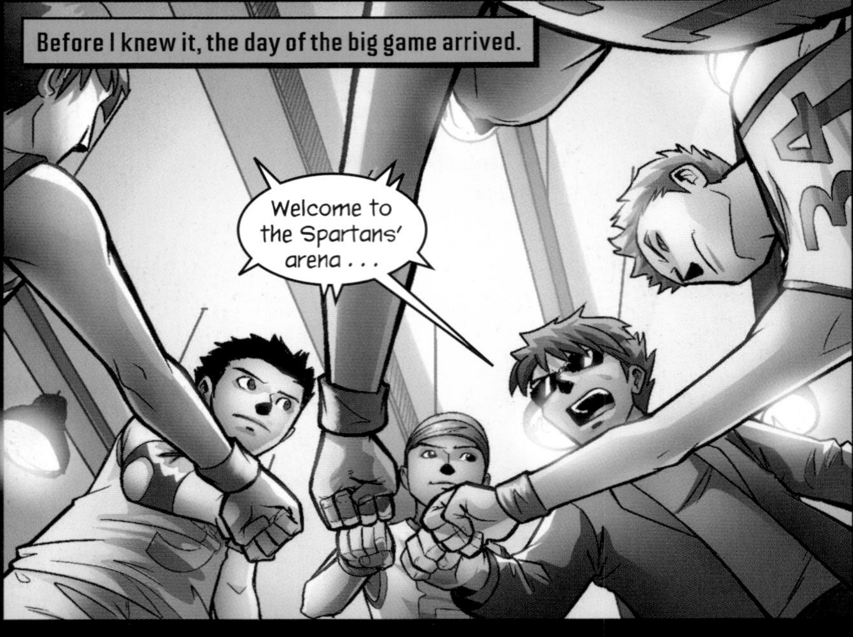
Before I knew it, the day of the big game arrived.
Welcome to the Spartans' arena . . .

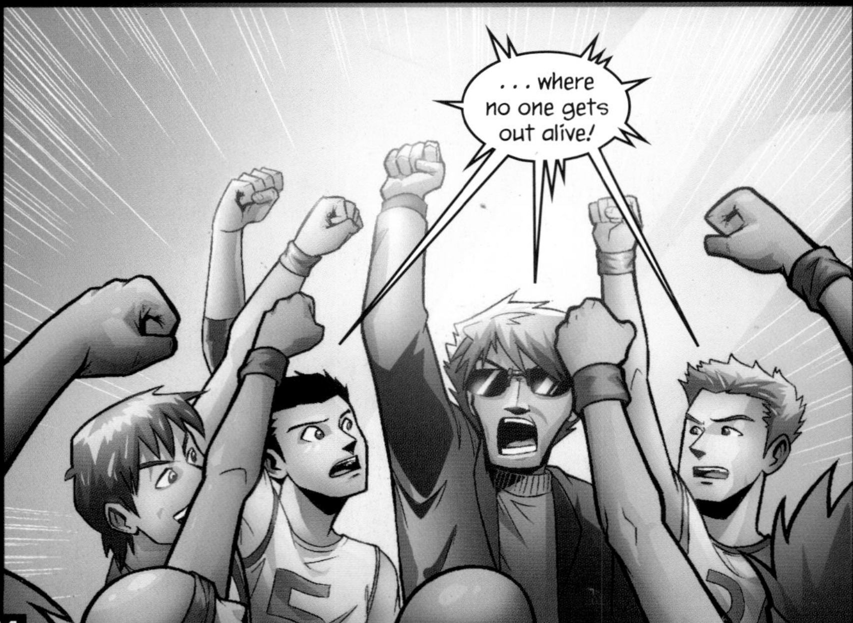
. . . where no one gets out alive!

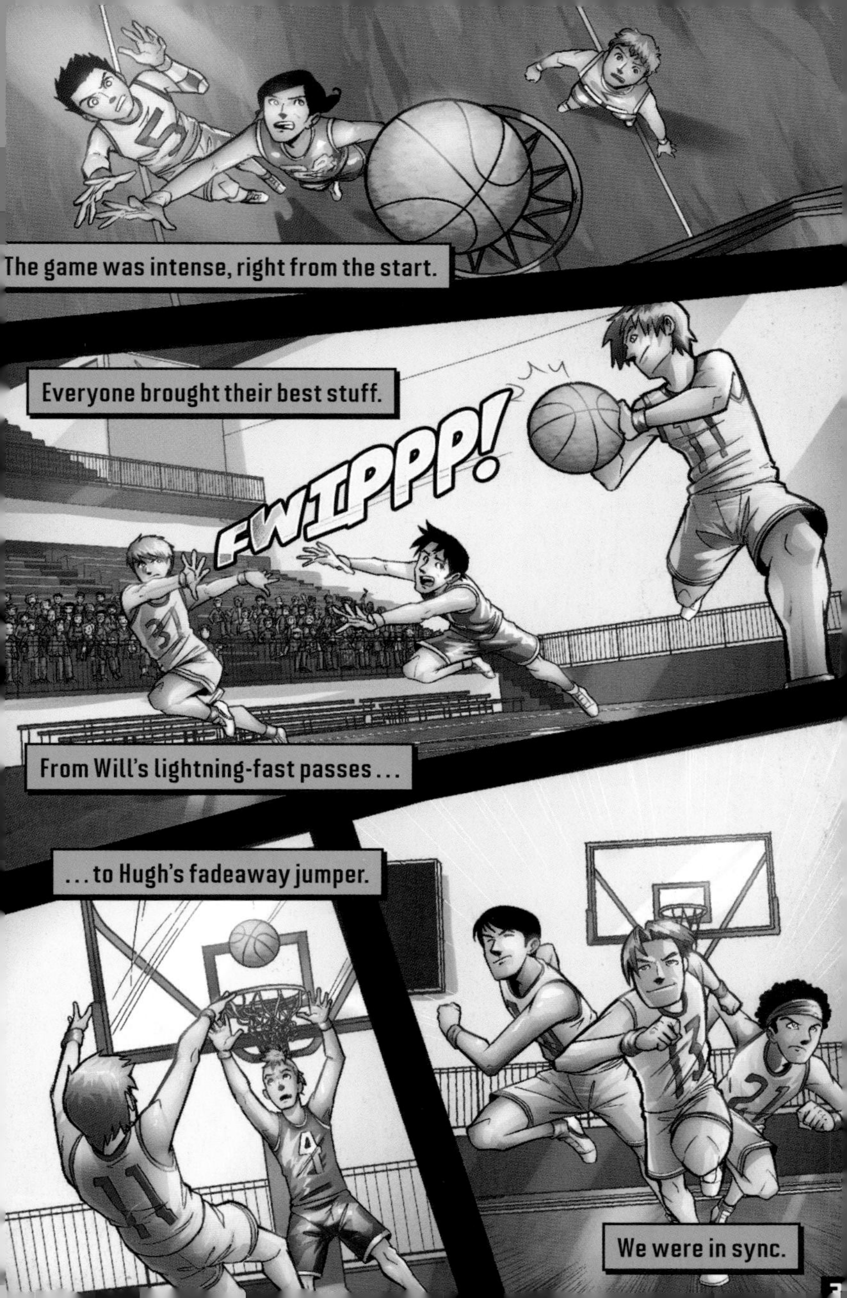

The game was intense, right from the start.
Everyone brought their best stuff.
FWIPPP!
From Will's lightning-fast passes . . .
. . . to Hugh's fadeaway jumper.
We were in sync.

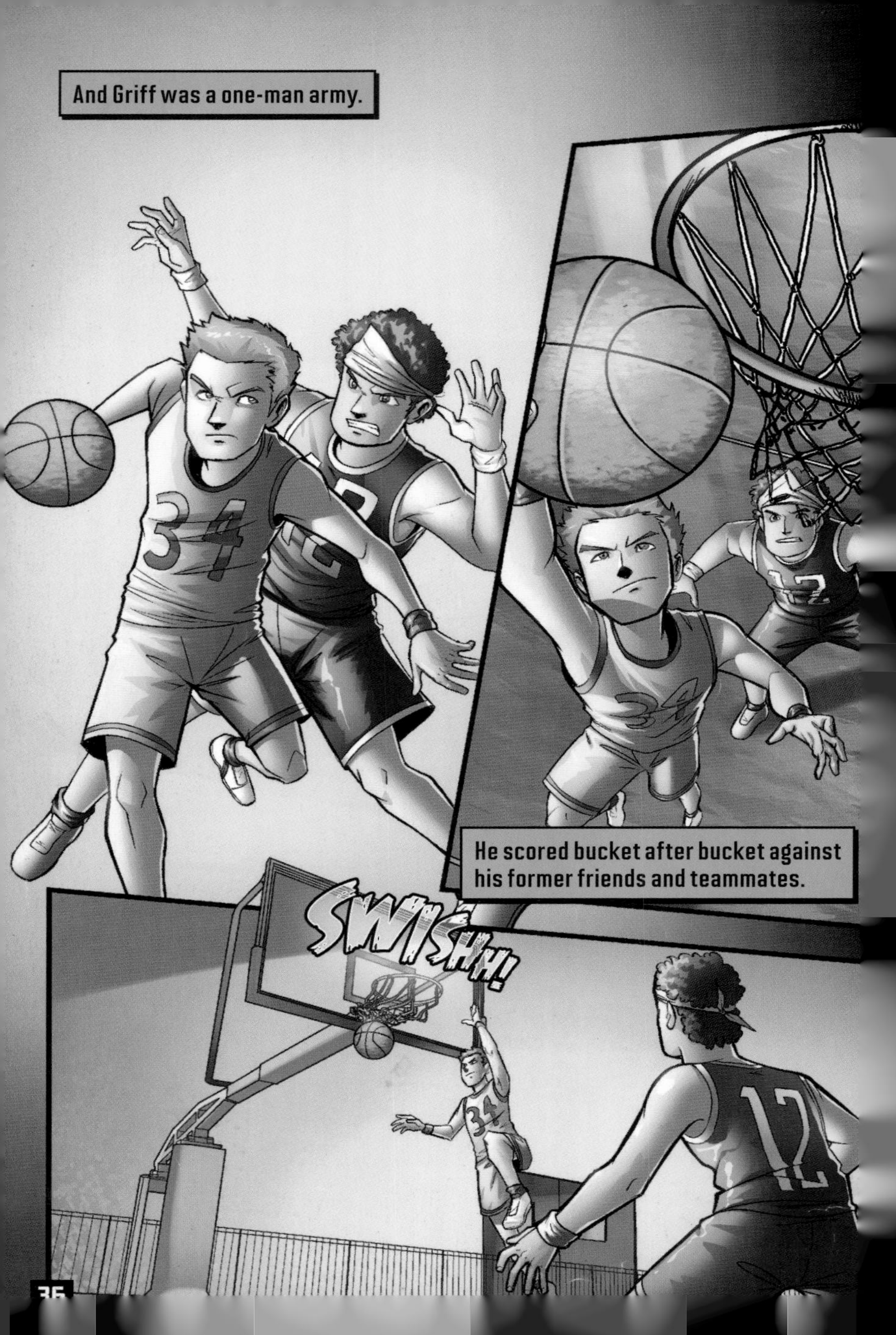
And Griff was a one-man army.
He scored bucket after bucket against his former friends and teammates.
SWISHH!

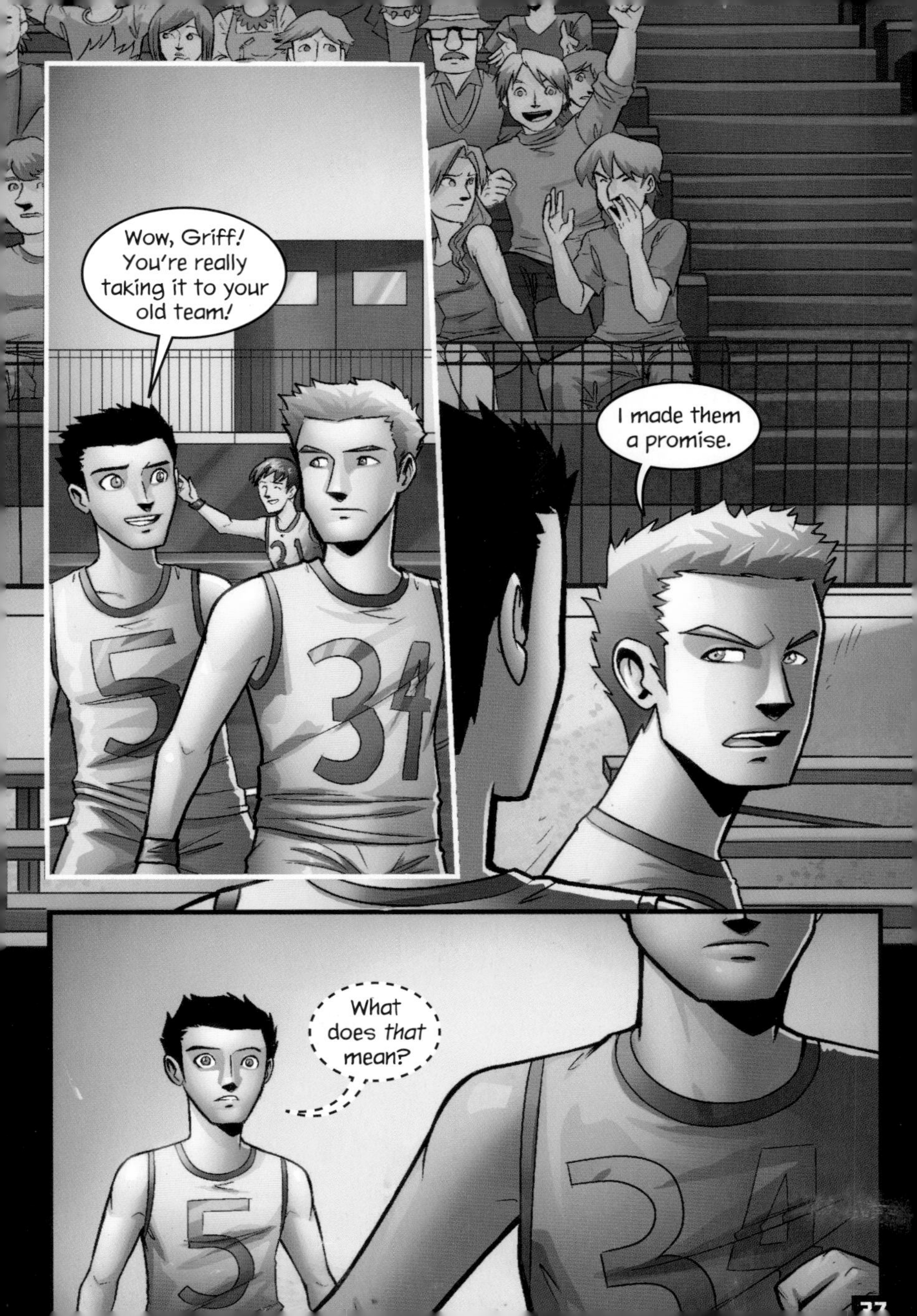

Wow, Griff! You're really taking it to your old team!
I made them a promise.
What does that mean?

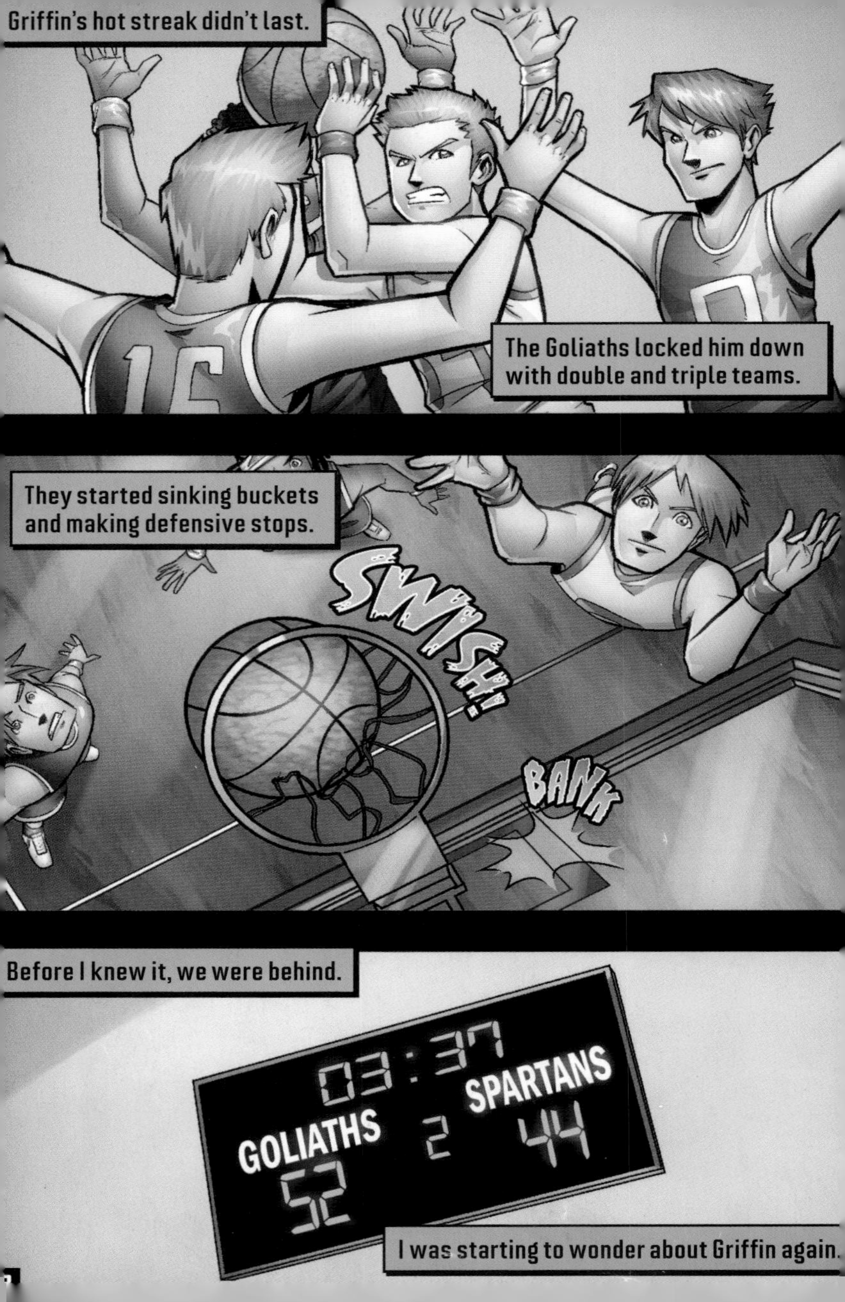
Griffin's hot streak didn't last.
The Goliaths locked him down with double and triple teams.
They started sinking buckets and making defensive stops.
SWISH!
BANK
Before I knew it, we were behind.
03:37
GOLIATHS
52
2
SPARTANS
44
I was starting to wonder about Griffin again.

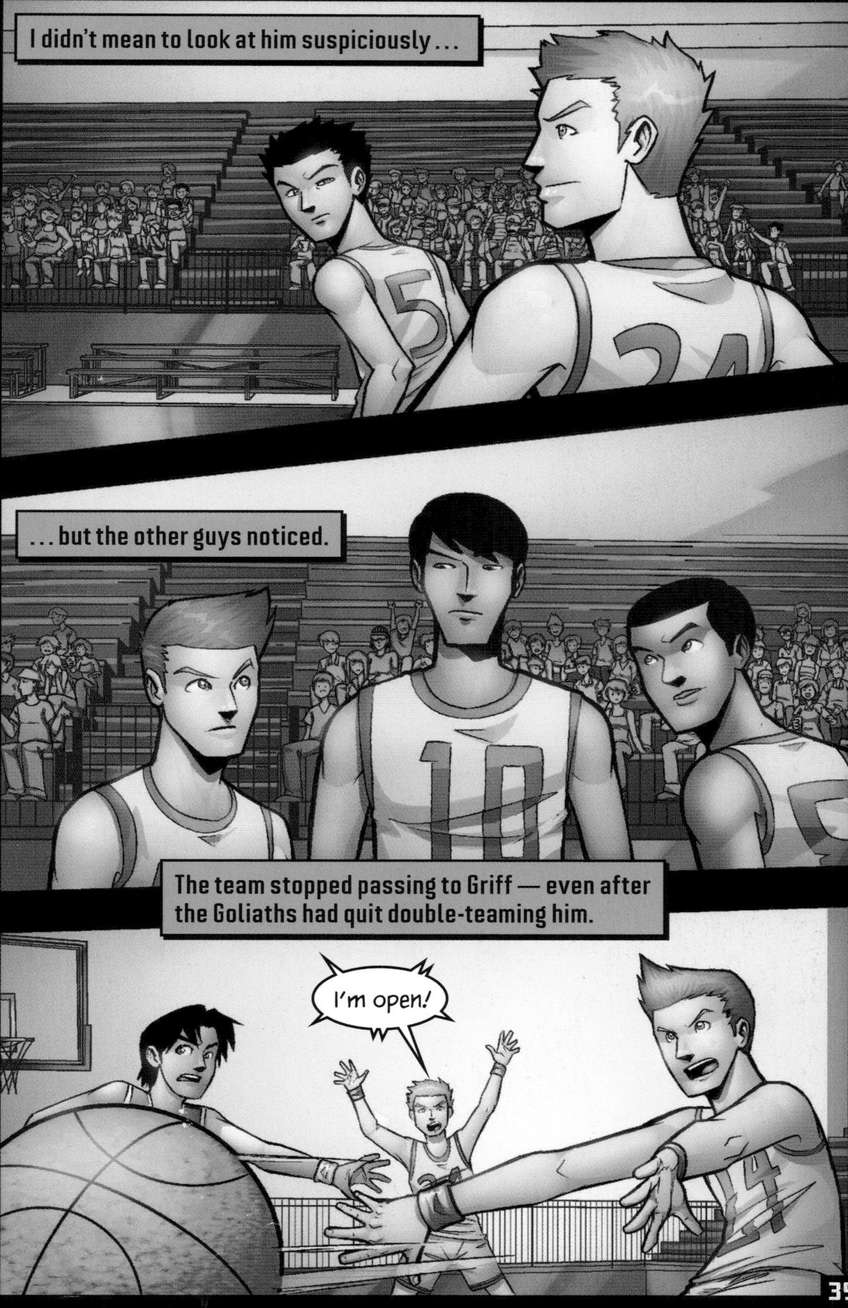
I didn't mean to look at him suspiciously . . .
. . . but the other guys noticed.
The team stopped passing to Griff — even after the Goliaths had quit double-teaming him.
I'm open!

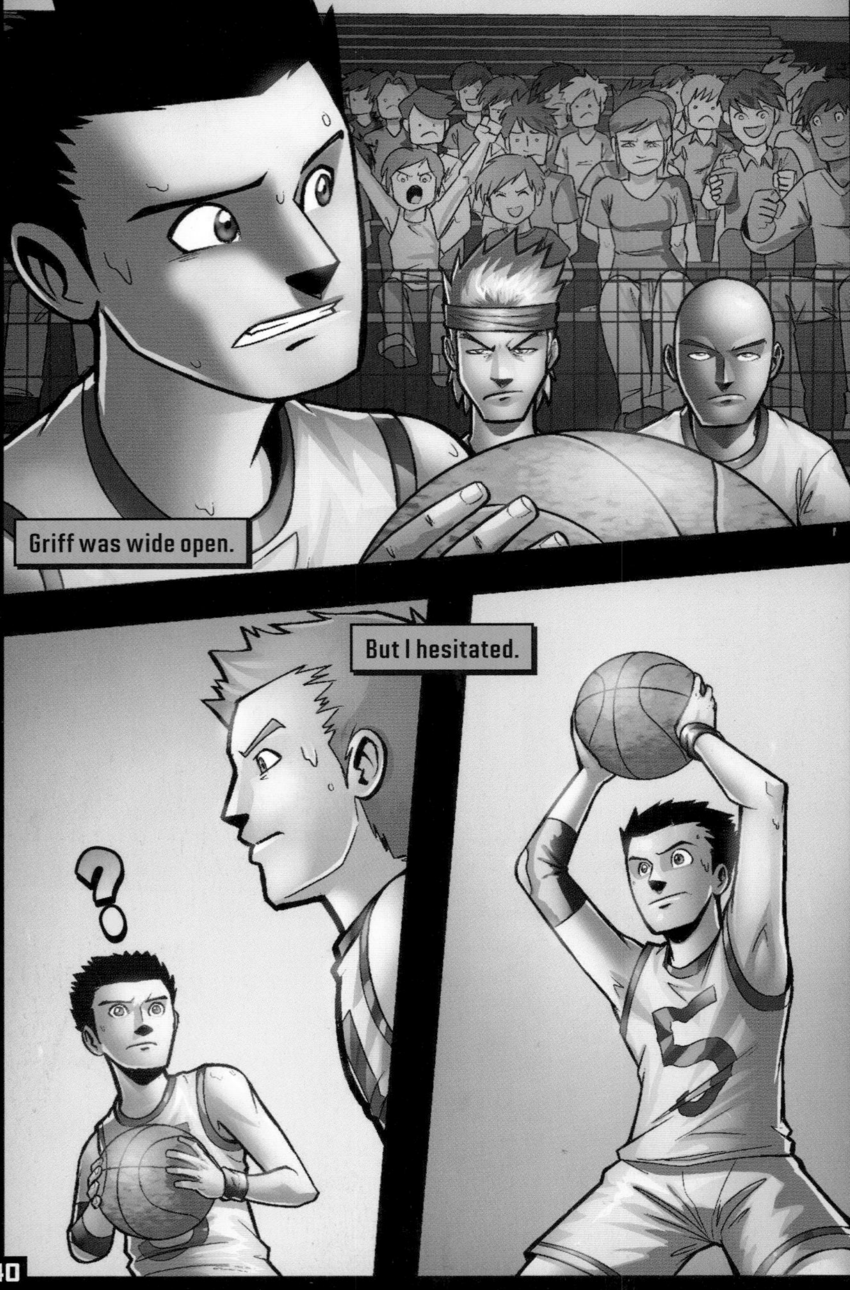
Griff was wide open.
But I hesitated.
?

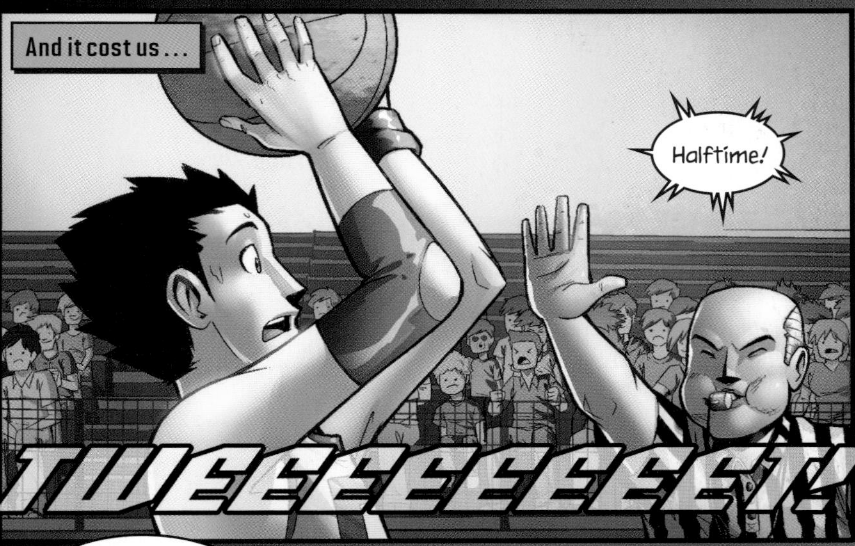
And it cost us . . .
Halftime!
TWEEEEEEET!

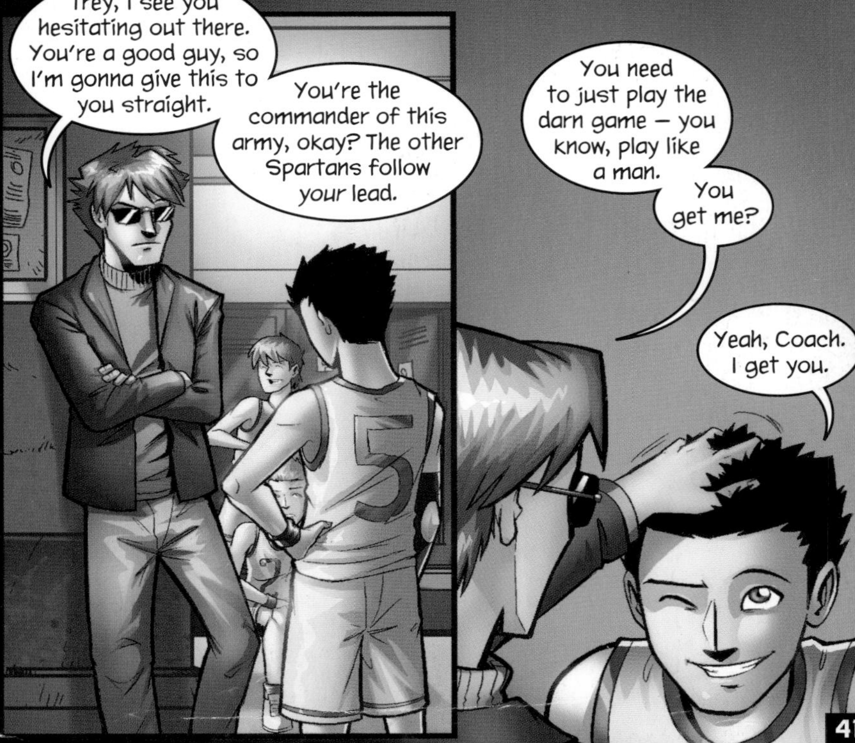
Trey, I see you hesitating out there. You're a good guy, so I'm gonna give this to you straight.
You're the commander of this army, okay? The other Spartans follow *your* lead.
You need to just play the darn game — you know, play like a man.
You get me?
Yeah, Coach. I get you.

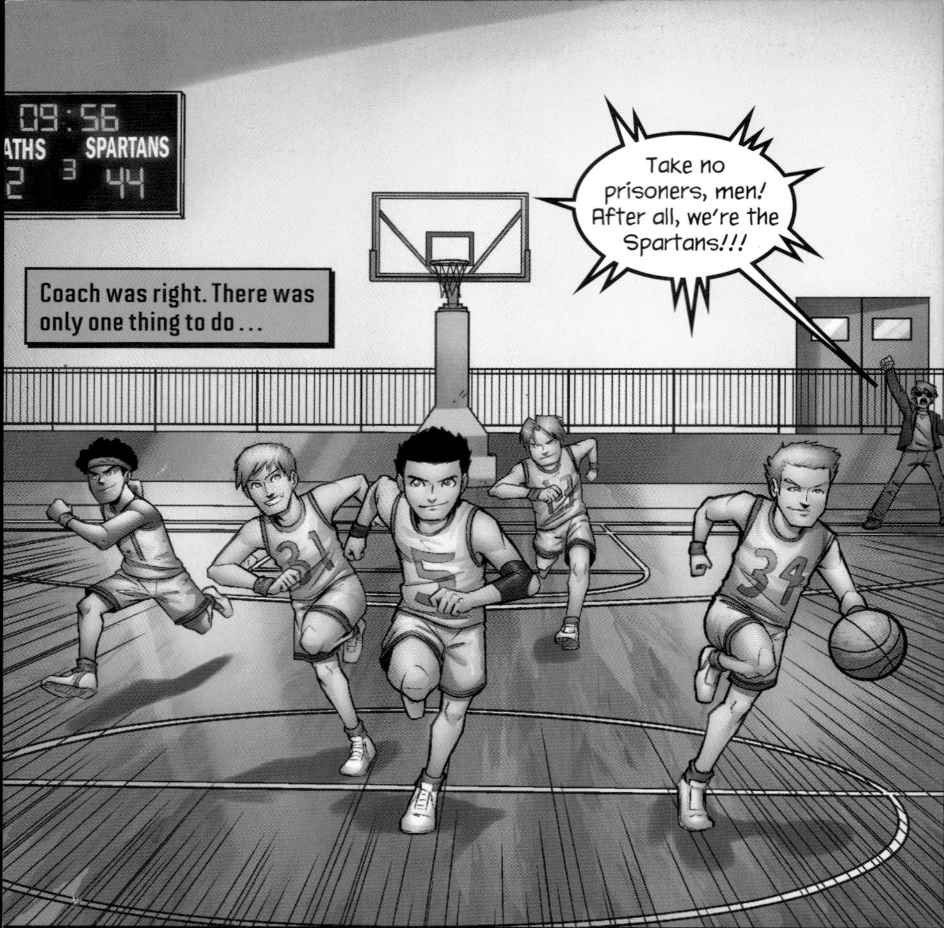
09:56
ATHS SPARTANS
2 3 44
Coach was right. There was only one thing to do . . .
Take no prisoners, men! After all, we're the Spartans!!!

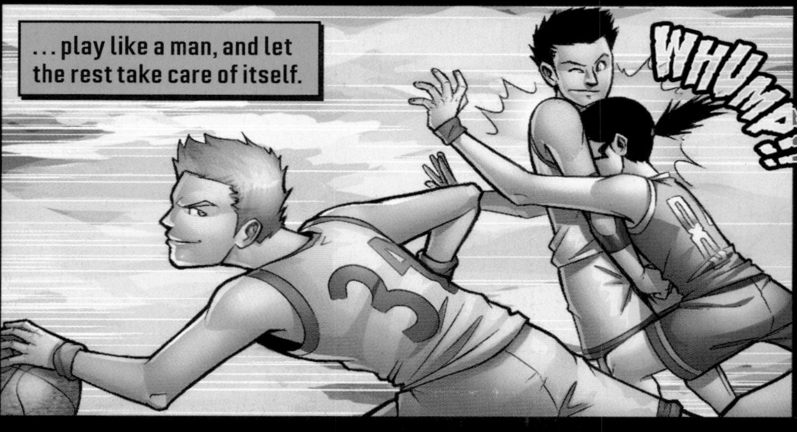
. . . play like a man, and let the rest take care of itself.
WHUMP!!

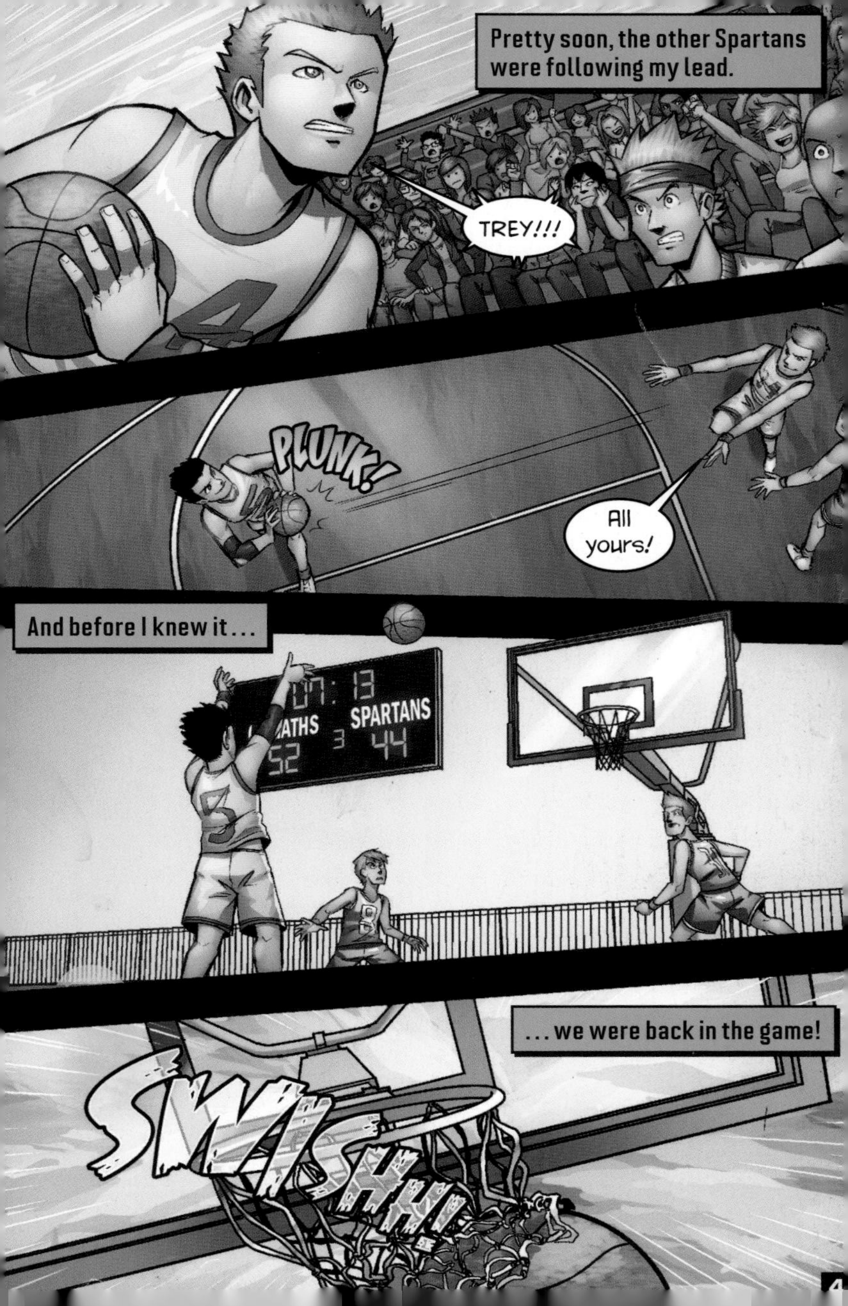
Pretty soon, the other Spartans were following my lead.
TREY!!!
PLUNK!
All yours!
And before I knew it . . .
SPARTANS
52
44
. . . we were back in the game!
SWISHH!

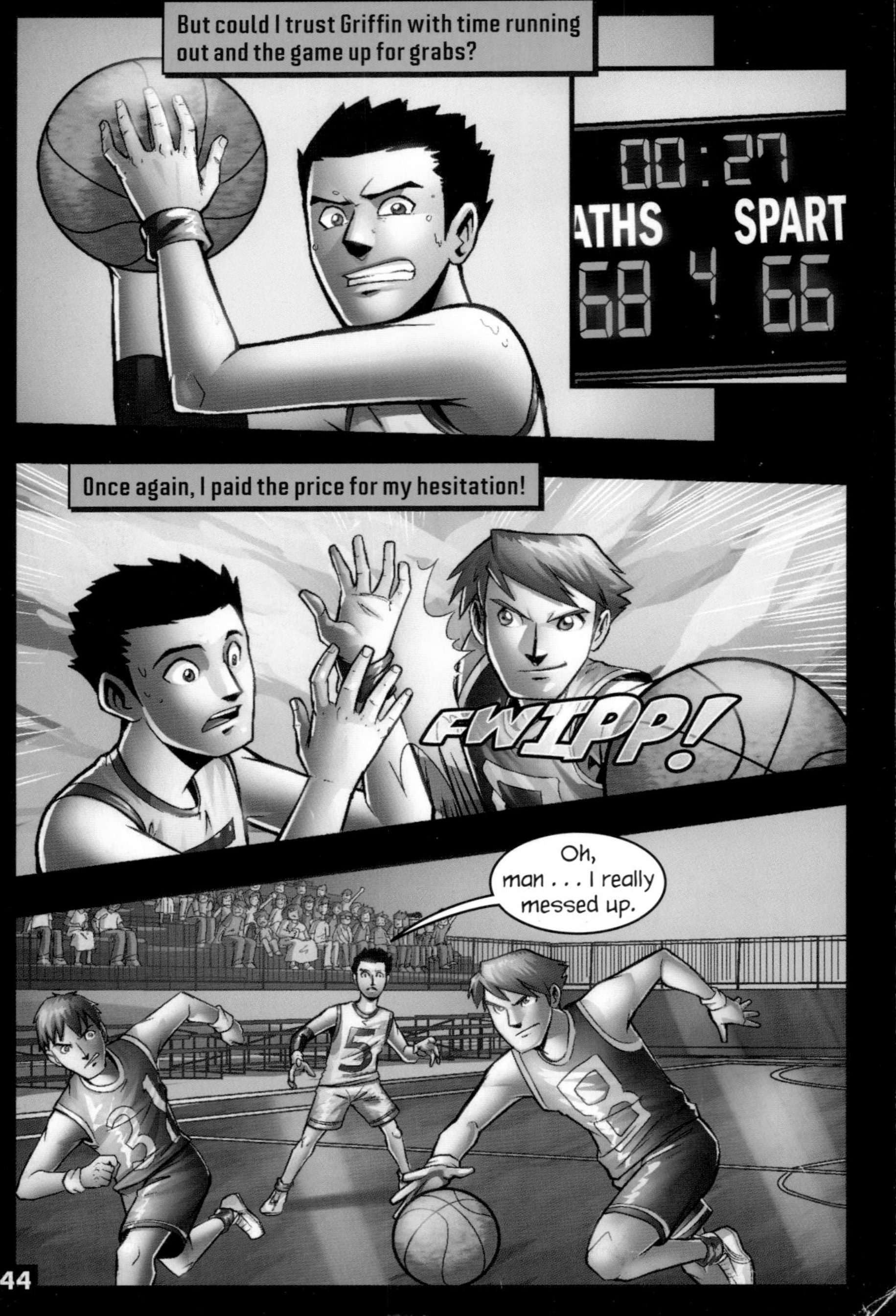
But could I trust Griffin with time running out and the game up for grabs?
00:27
ATHS SPART
68 4 66
Once again, I paid the price for my hesitation!
FWIPP!
Oh, man . . . I really messed up.

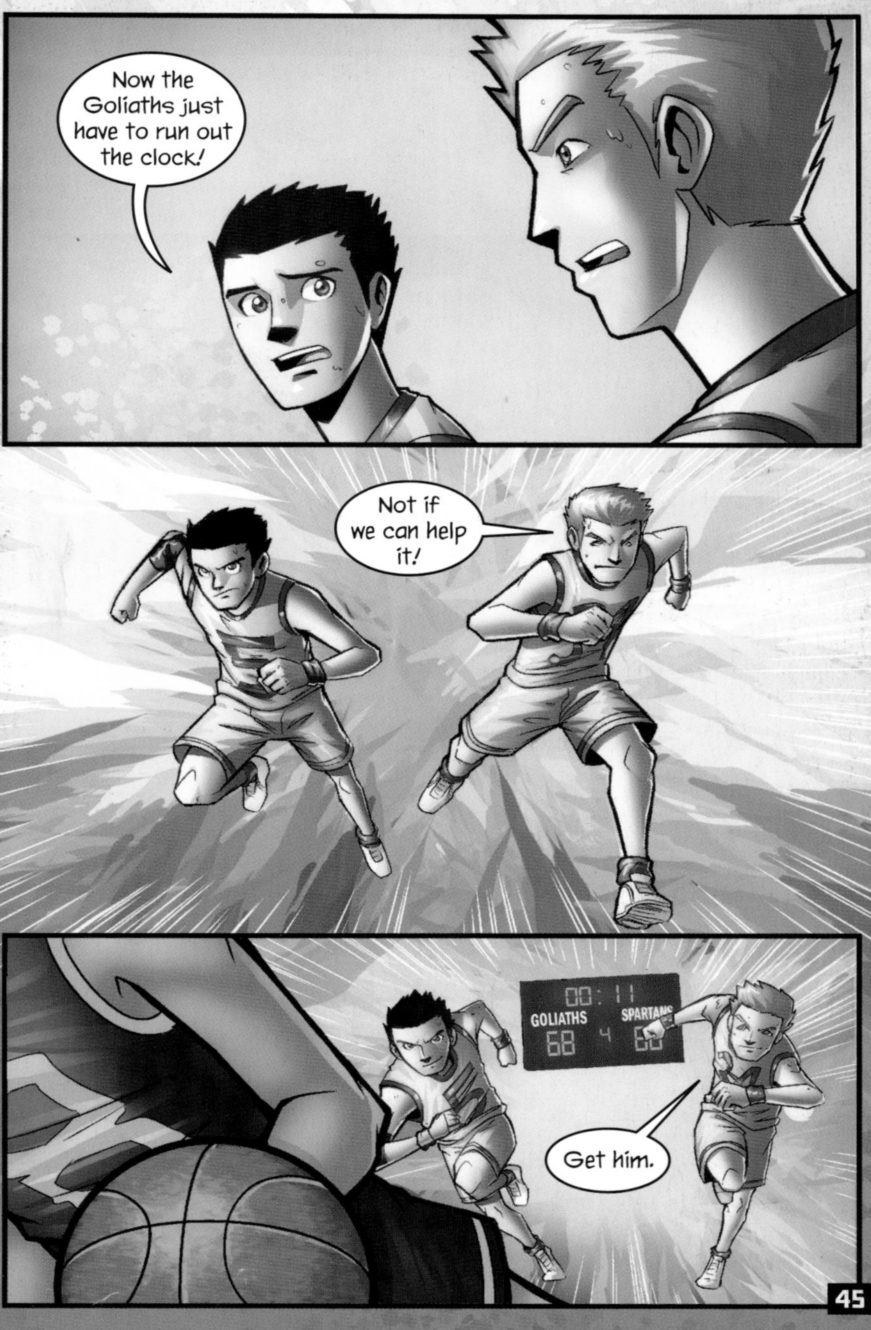
Now the Goliaths just have to run out the clock!
Not if we can help it!
00:11
GOLIATHS
SPARTANS
68
4
Get him.

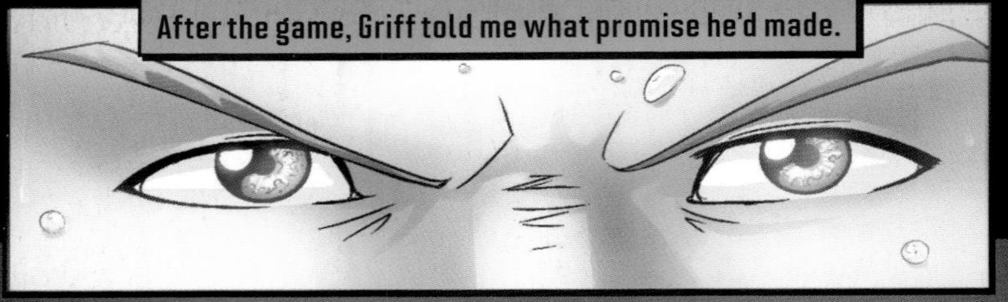
After the game, Griff told me what promise he'd made.

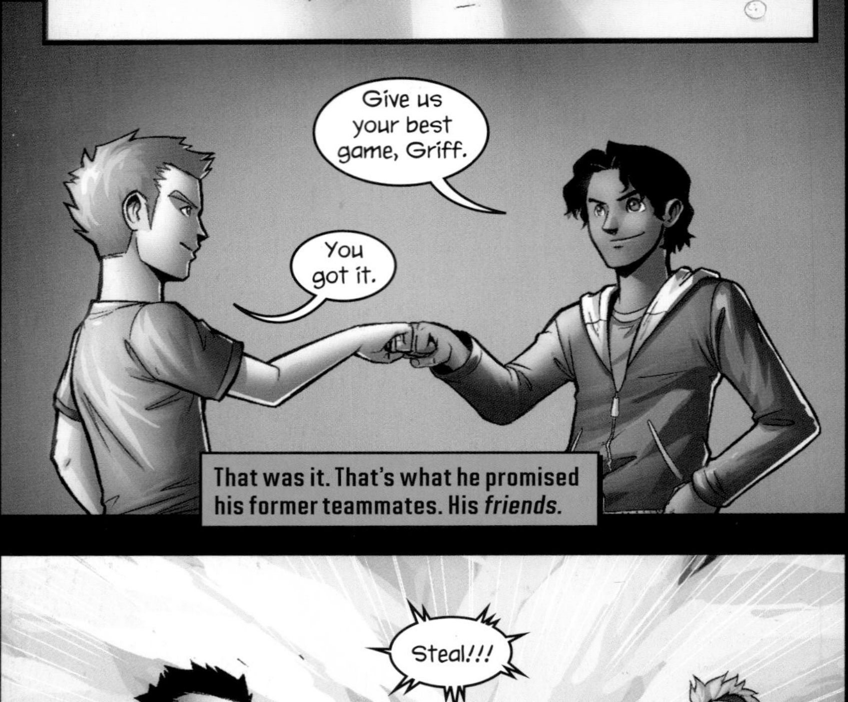
Give us your best game, Griff.
You got it.
That was it. That's what he promised his former teammates. His *friends.*

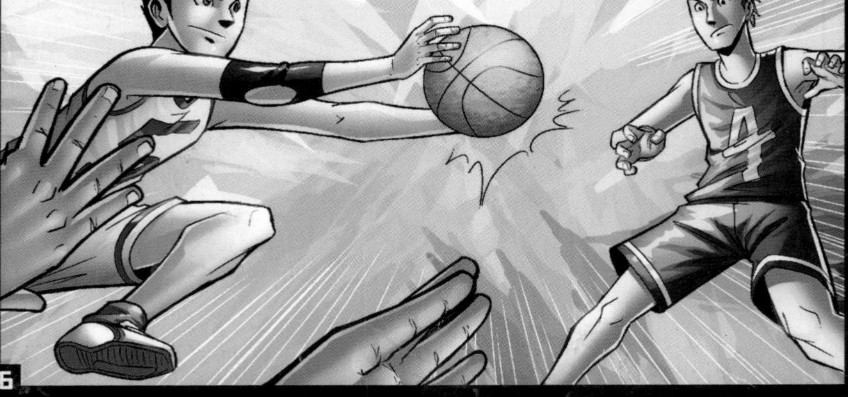
Steal!!!

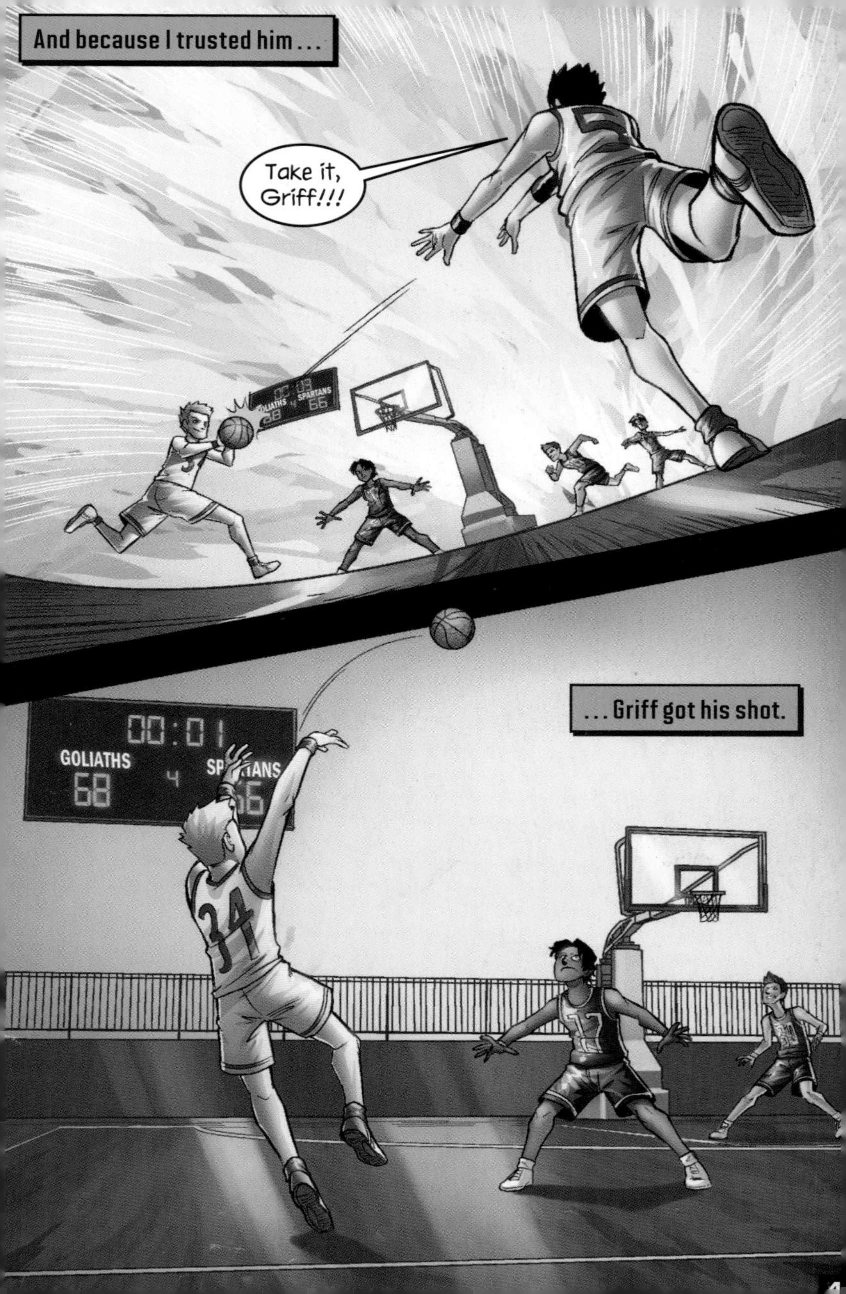
And because I trusted him . . .
Take it, Griff!!!
GOLIATHS
SPARTANS
00:01
GOLIATHS
68
4
66
. . . Griff got his shot.

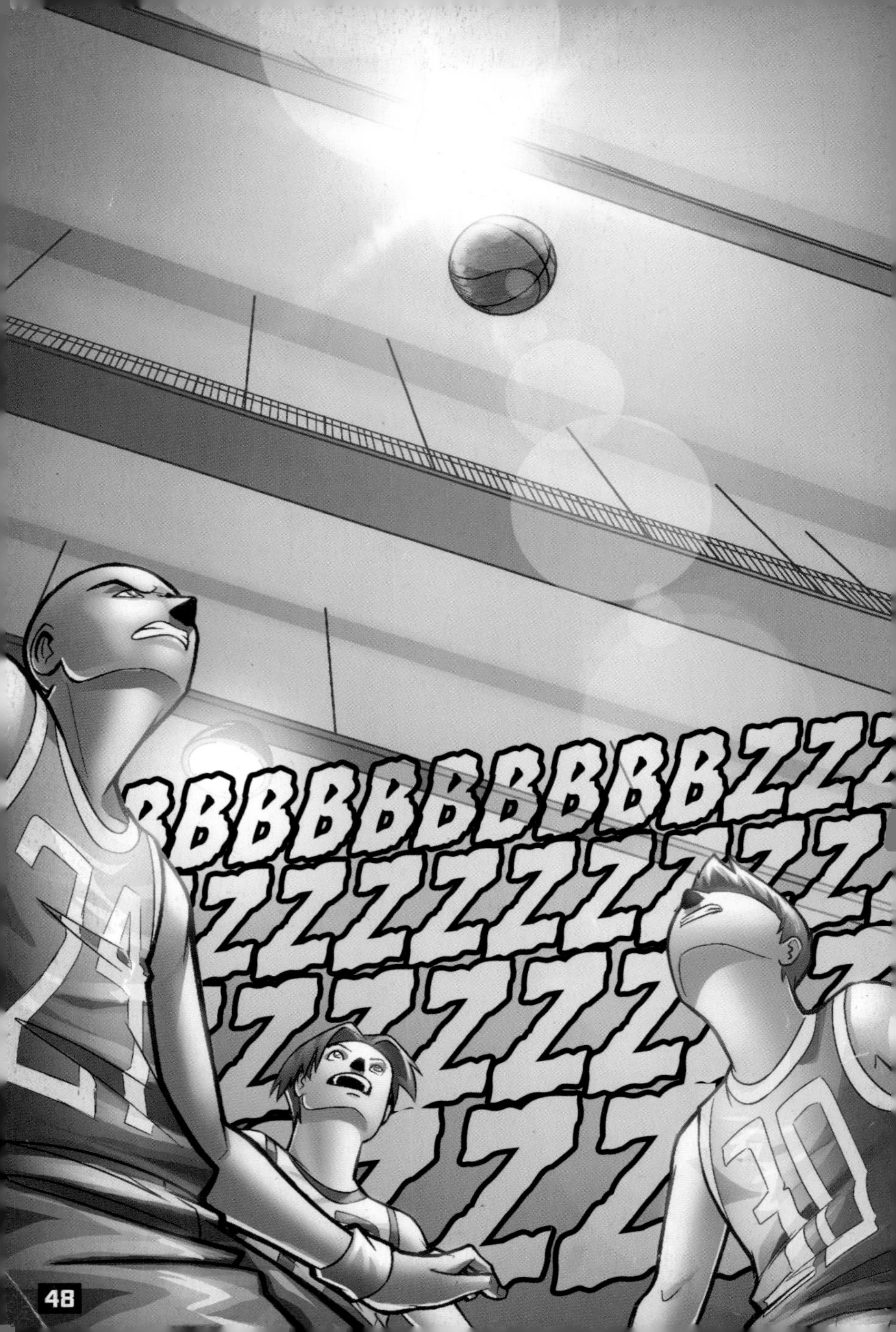
BBBBBBBBBZZZZZZZZZZZZZZZ

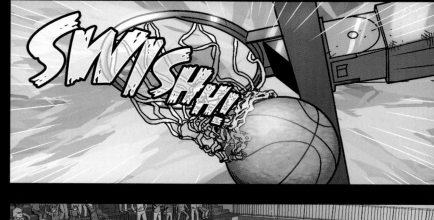

Yeah!!!

Way to go, Spartans!

Sushi's on me, guys!

Like I said — Griffin's got guts.

SPORTS ZONE
POSTGAME RECAP

BBL
BASKETBALL

PNT
PAINTBALL

FBL
FOOTBALL

BSL
BASEBALL

SOC
SOCCER

HKY

SPARTANS RALLY TOGETHER TO OVERCOME GOLIATHS

BY THE NUMBERS

STAT LEADERS:
POINTS: GRIFFIN, 33
ASSISTS: TREY, 11
BLOCKS: JAY, 4

STORY: The Spartans were convinced a rat was on their team — and that his name was Griffin Henshaw. But as the game against the Goliaths went on, the Spartans realized that Griff was on their side — he torched his former team for 33 points! Trey McTiernan said, "Once we saw how committed Griff was to playing his best against his friends, we knew he was a Spartan at heart."

UP NEXT: SI KIDS INFO CENTER

SZ POSTGAME EXTRA

WHERE **YOU** ANALYZE THE GAME!

BLZ vs BHS
3-1
TGR vs ROR
33-32
EAG vs BAN
14-7
SPA vs WLD
4-3
BAN vs ROR
21-15
RZR vs LIG
4-3
BLZ vs BHS
3-1

Basketball fans got a real treat today when the Spartans faced off against the Goliaths. Let's go into the stands and ask some fans for their opinions on the day's big game...

DISCUSSION QUESTION 1

Should trust be given or earned? Do you trust people right away, or does it take a while? Why?

DISCUSSION QUESTION 2

Who is your favorite Spartan? Griff, Trey, Max, Coach Schu? Why?

WRITING PROMPT 1

Are there any other ways that Trey could've found out whether or not Griffin could be trusted? Write down some methods for Trey to test Griff's loyalty.

WRITING PROMPT 2

Have you ever had to move to a new place? What do you think would be difficult about changing schools? Write about it.

Sports Illustrated KIDS

INFO CENTER

GLOSSARY

ANTICIPATE (an-TISS-i-pate)—to expect something to happen and be prepared for it

COCKY (KOK-ee)—overconfident or too sure of oneself

FADEAWAY (FAYD-uh-way)—a type of jump shot where the shooter fades backward while releasing the ball

FATE (FATE)—what will happen

HESITATION (hez-uh-TAY-shuhn)—pausing or waiting due to uncertainty

INTENSE (in-TENSS)—very strong and unrelenting

RAT (RAT)—a spy, or a disloyal and untrustworthy person

SUSHI (SOO-shee)—a Japanese dish made of raw fish or seafood that is pressed into special rice

SUSPICIOUS (suh-SPISH-uhss)—if you feel suspicious, you think that something seems wrong

SYNC (SINK)—if you are in sync with someone, then you are working together perfectly with that person

CREATORS

Scott Ciencin › Author

Scott Ciencin is a *New York Times* bestselling author of children's and adult fiction. He has written comic books, trading cards, video games, television shows, as well as many non-fiction projects. He lives in Sarasota, Florida with his beloved wife, Denise, and his best buddy, Bear, a golden retriever.

Aburtov › Managing Illustrator

Aburtov runs his own illustration studio called Graphikslava, where he manages many talented illustrators ...

Fernando Cano › Penciler

Fernando Cano is an emerging illustrator born in Mexico City, Mexico. He currently works as a full-time illustrator and colorist at Graphikslava studio. He has done illustration work for Marvel, DC Comics, and role-playing games like *Pathfinder* from Paizo Publishing. In his spare time, he enjoys hanging out with friends, singing, rowing, and drawing!

Andres Esparza › Inker

Andres Esparza has been a graphic designer, colorist, and illustrator for many different companies and agencies. Andres now works as a full-time artist for Graphikslava studio in Monterrey, Mexico. In his spare time, Andres loves to play basketball, hang out with family and friends, and listen to good music.

Fares Maese › Colorist

Fares Maese is a graphic designer and illustrator. He has worked as a colorist for Marvel Comics, and as a concept artist for the card and role-playing games *Pathfinder* and *Warhammer*. Fares loves spending time playing video games with his Graphikslava comrades, and he's an awesome drum player.

Sports Illustrated KIDS GRAPHIC NOVELS
QUICK COMIC

DASH the FLASH IN: FULL COURT FLASH

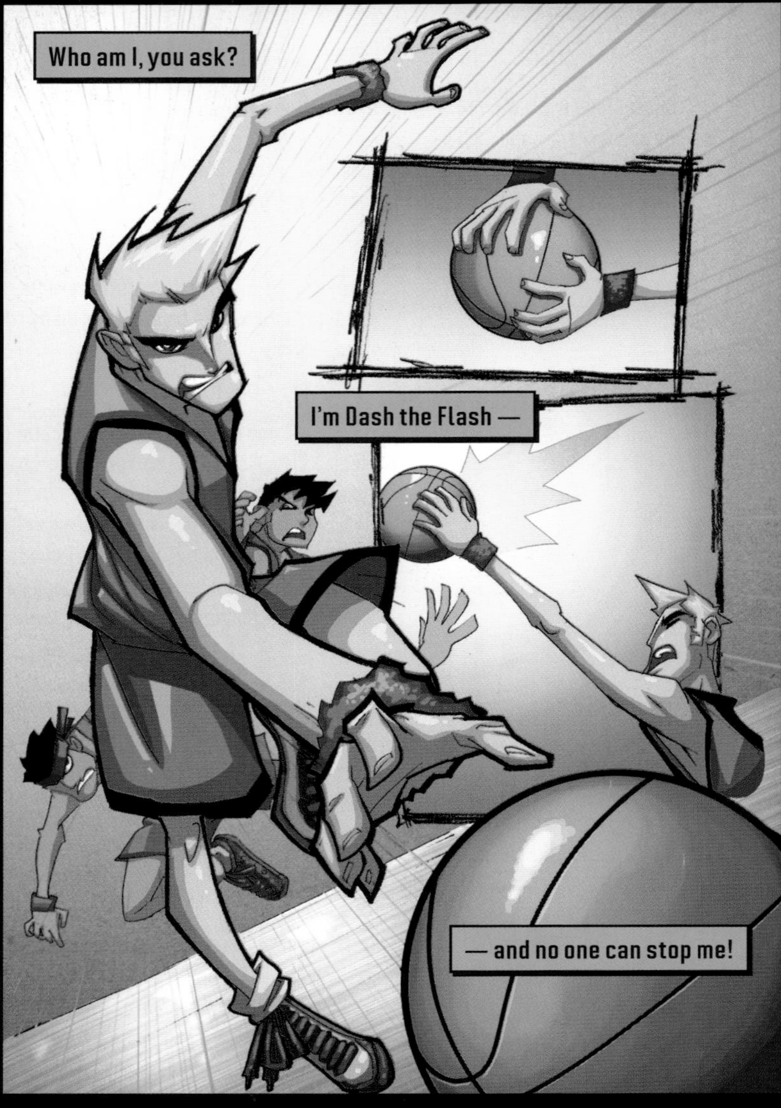
Who am I, you ask?
I'm Dash the Flash —
— and no one can stop me!

» LOVE THIS QUICK COMIC? READ THE WHOLE STORY IN FULL COURT FLASH – ONLY FROM STONE ARCH BOOKS!

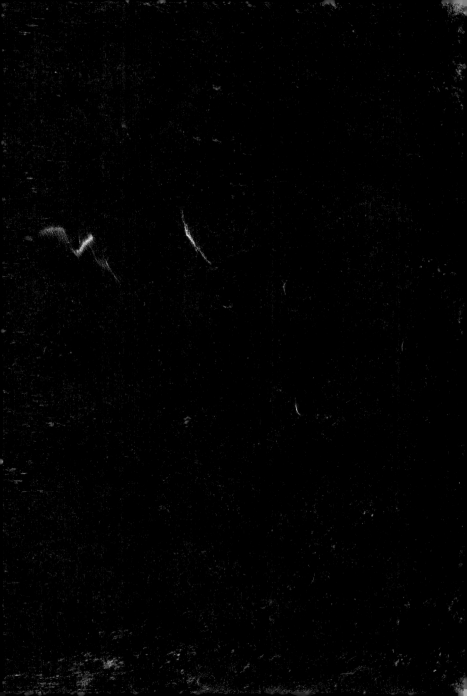

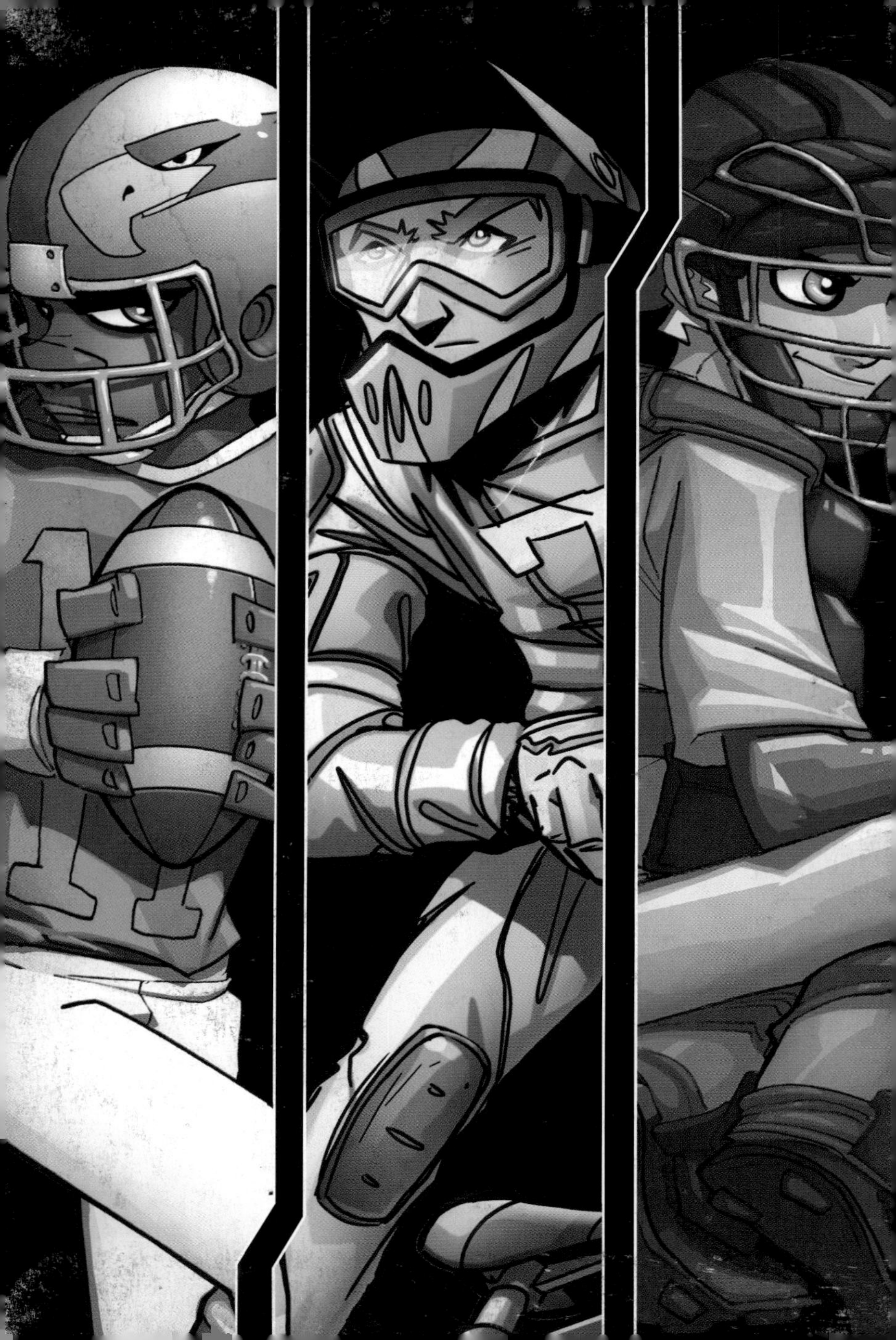